"Please hold me."

That was the only warning Jax got before Paige was in his arms.

Instant jolt of memories. His body reminding him that it'd been way too long since he'd had her in his arms.

And in his bed.

Jax didn't push her away, though. She was falling apart right in front of him, and he felt his arms close around her before he could talk himself out of it.

"I'm sorry," she said.

The latest apology put his teeth on edge. No way could an apology erase what she'd done. For nearly a year, he'd grieved for her. Cursed her. Because he'd believed she had caused her own death. Now he was cursing her for lying to him. Cursing her because of this blasted attraction that just wouldn't die.

SIX-GUN SHOWDOWN

USA TODAY Bestselling Author

DELORES FOSSEN

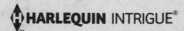
HARLEQUIN INTRIGUE®

Recycling programs
for this product may
not exist in your area.

ISBN-13: 978-0-373-69920-9

Six-Gun Showdown

Printed in U.S.A.

Delores Fossen, a *USA TODAY* bestselling author, has sold over fifty novels with millions of copies of her books in print worldwide. She's received a Booksellers' Best Award and an RT Reviewers' Choice Best Book Award. She was also a finalist for a prestigious RITA® Award. You can contact the author through her website at deloresfossen.com.

Books by Delores Fossen

Harlequin Intrigue

Appaloosa Pass Ranch

Lone Wolf Lawman
Taking Aim at the Sheriff
Trouble with a Badge
The Marshal's Justice
Six-Gun Showdown

Sweetwater Ranch

Maverick Sheriff
Cowboy Behind the Badge
Rustling Up Trouble
Kidnapping in Kendall County
The Deputy's Redemption
Reining in Justice
Surrendering to the Sheriff
A Lawman's Justice

HQN Books

The McCord Brothers

Texas on My Mind
Lone Star Nights

Visit the Author Profile page at Harlequin.com for more titles.

CAST OF CHARACTERS

Deputy Jax Crockett—Nearly a year ago, he thought his ex-wife, Paige, had been murdered by a serial killer. But now Paige is back, and Jax has no choice but to push their painful past aside and stop the killer from coming after her again.

Paige Crockett—When she faked her death, she thought it would save Jax and their son from the serial killer, but she was dead wrong. And now they're all in danger.

Matthew Crockett—Jax and Paige's two-year-old son. He has no idea how much his parents are willing to sacrifice for him.

The Moonlight Strangler—A vicious serial killer who left Paige for dead. Is he after her again, or is someone pretending to be him?

Cord Granger—He's the Moonlight Strangler's biological son and would do anything to put his father behind bars.

Darrin Pittman—Rich, pampered and out for revenge because he claims Paige planted evidence against him.

Leland Fountain—A San Antonio cop who helped Paige fake her death, but he's also developed feelings for her.

Belinda Darby—Matthew's nanny. She's in love with Jax and isn't happy about Paige's return.

Chapter One

I'm not dead.

The voice mail message caused Deputy Jax Crockett to freeze. He stabbed the replay button on his phone and listened to it again. Three words. That was it.

But it felt as if a stick of dynamite had just gone off in his chest.

Paige.

Oh, mercy. It was his ex-wife, Paige.

That was her voice, all right. He was sure of it. But it couldn't be her because he'd buried her a year ago.

Jax listened to the message again. And again. Then, he checked the name and number of the caller.

Unknown.

Which meant the person might have blocked him from seeing it. But it'd come in a half hour earlier when he'd been on the back part of his ranch looking for a calf that'd strayed from the herd. No phone reception was back there, so the call had gone straight to voice mail.

Was that fear he'd heard in her voice?

Or maybe fear that someone else was pretending to feel?

This had to be some kind of sick prank. That was it. Maybe someone who sounded like Paige.

But his gut didn't go along with that notion.

He knew his ex-wife's voice, and that'd been her on the other end of the line. Of course, that didn't mean someone hadn't used an old recording of her voice, perhaps piecing together words from other conversations to come up with that one sentence.

I'm not dead.

"You okay, boss?" he heard someone ask.

Jax dragged his thoughts back to reality and noticed that one of his ranch hands, Buddy Martindale, was looking at him as if he'd lost his mind.

Heck, maybe he had.

After all, he was standing in the barn while he repeatedly punched the voice mail button on his phone.

"Did anybody call the ranch in the past hour or so?" Jax asked him.

Buddy lifted his cowboy hat enough to scratch his head, giving that some thought. "Not that I know of. Maybe you oughta check with Belinda, though."

Yes, Belinda Darby would know. His son's nanny was inside the house, and since it was coming up on dinnertime, Belinda would be close to not only Jax's son, Matthew, but also near the house phone. She would have been able to hear the line ringing in Jax's home office, too, if someone had tried to reach him there.

Someone like a dead woman.

Get a grip.

Paige had been murdered by the serial killer known as the Moonlight Strangler. And there had to be some reasonable explanation for the call.

Jax handed off his horse's reins to Buddy, something he wouldn't normally do. Tending the horses was a task he enjoyed. Not today, though. Not after that message.

There were a good thirty yards between the barn and the back porch, so while he made his way to the house, Jax listened to the recording again. Hearing it for the fifth time didn't lessen the impact.

The memories came, slamming into him.

Nightmares of the violence Paige had suffered. Folks often reminded him that she'd only died once. That she wasn't suffering now, that she was at peace. And while that was true, Jax couldn't stop himself from reliving every last horrifying moment of Paige's life.

Their marriage had fallen apart several months before she was killed, but it didn't matter that their divorce had been finalized only days before that fateful night. Paige sure hadn't deserved to die, and their son hadn't deserved to lose his mother.

Before Jax reached the back porch, the door opened, and Belinda stuck out her head. Even though the sunset wasn't far off, it was still hot, the August air more humid than cooling, and the breeze took a swipe at her long blond hair.

"You look like you saw a ghost," she said, smiling, but that smile quickly vanished. "Is everything all right?"

Heck, he must have been wearing his emotions on his face and every other part of him. A rarity for him since, to the best of his knowledge, no one had ever called him the emotional type.

"Have there been any calls since I've been out?" he asked.

"No." Unlike Buddy, Belinda didn't even hesitate. "Why? What's wrong?"

Jax waved her off. No need to worry her. And she would be worried if he told her about the voice mail. Belinda took care of Matthew as if he were her own and would have done the same for Jax if he'd let her. Anything that bothered the two of them would bother her.

"Can you stay late tonight? I need to go back to the sheriff's office and look over some reports," he lied.

Well, it was sort of a lie, anyway. He was a deputy after all, and there were always reports to read, write or look over. He'd maybe work on a few while he was there.

But what he really wanted was to have the voice mail analyzed.

He'd saved the old answering machine with Paige's recorded message on it. Jax had figured when Matthew got older, he might want to hear his mommy's voice.

Or at least that's what Jax had told himself.

But now, the recording could be compared to the one on his voice mail, and he'd have the proof he needed that this was some kind of a sick hoax. Maybe then the knot in his stomach would ease up.

"No problem. I can stay as late as you need," Belinda assured him.

He hadn't expected her to say anything different. "Thanks. And don't hold dinner for me. I'll be back before Matthew's bedtime, though."

Belinda nodded and went back inside. But not before giving him another concerned look. She would believe his lie because she wanted to believe it, but she knew something was wrong.

Jax was within a few steps of the back porch when he caught some movement from the corner of his eye. Just a blur of motion in the open doorway of the detached garage. Since Buddy was still in the main barn, Jax knew it wasn't him, and none of the hands from his family's ranch had come to help him work today. Still, that didn't mean his sister or brothers hadn't sent someone over to get a vehicle or something.

Except it didn't feel like anything that ordinary.

Probably because of that voice mail.

He was armed, his Glock in his waist holster, and Jax slid his hand over it and started toward the garage.

There.

He saw the movement again.

Someone was definitely inside.

He'd made some enemies over the years. That came with the territory of being a lawman. But if someone had decided to bring a fight to his ranch, then the person could have already ambushed him.

Not exactly a thought to steady his nerves.

"Who's there?" he asked. Not a shout.

Jax kept his voice low enough so that Belinda or anyone in the house wouldn't necessarily hear him. But a person in the garage should.

He got no answer, and he glanced back at his house to make sure Belinda was still inside. She was. Jax considered firing off a text to warn her to get Matthew and herself away from the windows, but it might be overkill.

Or not.

He got another glimpse of the shadowy figure and decided to confront this head-on. Literally. Jax drew his gun and hurried to the entry. It was dark inside, but not so dark that he didn't see the person lurking behind the back end of one of the trucks.

"Paige?" Jax whispered.

He could have sworn everything stopped. His heartbeat. His breath. Maybe even time. But that standstill didn't last.

Because the person stepped out, not enough for him to fully see her, but Jax knew it was a woman.

"You got my message," she said. "I'm so sorry."

Paige. It was her. In the flesh.

Jax had a thousand emotions hit him at once. Relief. Mercy, there was a ton of relief, but it didn't last but a second or two before the other emotions took over: shock, disbelief and, yeah, anger.

Lots and lots of anger.

"Why?" he managed to say, though he wasn't sure how he could even speak with his throat clamped shut.

Paige cleared her throat, too. "Because it was necessary."

As answers went, it sucked, and he let her know that with the scowl he aimed at her. "Why?" he repeated.

She stepped from the shadows but didn't come closer to him. Still, it was close enough for him to confirm what he already knew.

This was Paige.

She was back from the grave. Or else, back from a lie that she'd apparently let him believe.

For a *dead* woman, she didn't look bad, but she had changed. No more blond hair. It was dark brown now and cut short and choppy. She'd also lost some of those curves that'd always caught his eye and every other man's in town.

"I know you have a thousand questions," she said, rubbing her hands along the outside legs of her jeans. She also glanced around. Behind him.

Behind her.

"Just one question. Why the hell did you let me believe you were dead?" But Jax couldn't even wait for the answer. He cursed. "I saw pictures of you after the Moonlight Strangler had gotten his hands on you.

There's no reason you should have let me believe that'd happened to you."

"It *did* happen." She stepped even closer, and thanks to the sunlight spearing through the door, he saw the scar on her cheek.

The crescent-shaped knife cut that the Moonlight Strangler had given all his victims.

There were marks on her throat, too. Scars from the piano wire that had sliced into her skin when the killer strangled her.

"Yes." Paige touched her fingers to her neck. "It's healed now. For the most part."

She was wrong. It would never heal. Never go away. Not in his mind, anyway.

"But clearly you're not dead," he snapped. And he didn't want her to be, but he damn sure wanted some answers. "I've been through hell for the past year. *Hell*," Jax emphasized. "You didn't just put me through this, either. Matthew went through it, too."

Even though his son had been only a year old when Paige died, it'd broken Jax's heart to hear his son call out for his ma-ma.

"Matthew." Her breath hitched, and tears sprang to her eyes. "I did this for him. For you."

"You didn't do anything for me." There was no way for him to rein in the anger in his voice or any other part of him. "You let me believe you'd been murdered."

She nodded, came even closer. So close that he caught her familiar scent. But she also glanced around again.

"Because if I hadn't let you believe that, the Moonlight Strangler would have come after me again. And I was afraid he'd use Matthew and you to get to me."

He cursed again, dismissing that. "I'm a deputy sheriff."

"And that didn't stop him from getting to me," Paige reminded him just as quickly.

Good grief, she might as well have slugged him with a two-by-four. Because it was the truth. And it was a truth that Jax had struggled with for the past year.

He hadn't managed to save her.

But someone obviously had.

"What happened?" he demanded.

She paused, gathered her breath. Maybe her thoughts, too. "By the time the San Antonio cops got to the crime scene, I was barely alive. In fact, the first cop on the scene did report me as dead. That's the report that went out to you and everybody else. But the paramedics managed to revive me in the ambulance on the way to the hospital. I knew if word got out that I was alive, the killer would just come after me again."

He mentally went through all the details and saw one big question at the end of that explanation. "Who helped you come up with this stupid plan?"

"*I* came up with it." She glanced around again. "And I convinced a cop at SAPD who knew about me to go along with it."

Jax didn't miss the glancing around, nor the hesitation in her voice.

"Who helped you?" he pressed.

She dodged his gaze. "Other than the cop, Cord Granger helped."

Jax would have cursed again if he could have gotten his jaw unclenched. Cord Granger, a DEA agent. Also the biological brother to his adopted sister, Addie.

Cord and Addie's father was none other than the Moonlight Strangler himself. Though the law didn't have the actual identity of the vicious serial killer, they knew from DNA comparisons that both Cord and Addie were his biological children. Children the killer had abandoned when they were a little more than toddlers, and neither had any recollections of the man.

Too bad.

If they had a name, then they could find and arrest the piece of slime.

Something that Cord had made his top priority.

Jax had never cared much for Cord. And this wouldn't help. Because Cord was much more concerned about catching his birth father than he was with the safety of the people around him. Jax wouldn't have put it past the man to actually use Paige to draw the killer out. And now he'd apparently put Paige up to lying to him.

Not just any old lie, either.

But one that'd crushed Jax and the rest of his family.

"You were a fool to trust Cord," he finally managed to say. Jax shoved his thumb against his chest. "You should have trusted me instead."

She huffed. Not an angry sound, but more like stating the obvious. "We weren't exactly in a good place, Jax."

That was the wrong thing to say. A new wave of anger came. "You're sure you didn't *die* because you didn't want to face the divorce?" Or maybe because she hadn't wanted to face him?

Her eyes narrowed when their gazes connected again. "No. It was to save Matthew and you."

Jax didn't have time to figure out if he believed that or not. Because he heard something he didn't want to hear.

Belinda's voice.

"Jax, are you all right?" the nanny called out.

Belinda was on the back porch, peering into the garage. She could almost certainly see him, but probably not Paige. Paige kept it that way by stepping into the shadows.

"Tell her to go back inside," Paige insisted.

Jax opened his mouth to ask why, but because he was watching Paige so closely, he saw the urgency slide across her face.

And the fear.

"I'm fine," he told Belinda. "Just checking a few things before I head to the office."

He waited to see if that'd be enough or if he truly would have to tell her to go inside. But thankfully, it worked. Belinda went back in and closed the door.

"What happened?" Jax asked Paige. And he didn't need his lawman's instincts to tell him that not only had something happened…

Something had gone wrong.

"What made you come back now?" he pressed.

The fear in her face went up a significant notch. "I think the Moonlight Strangler is on his way here to draw me out."

All right. That upped his concern, too. A lot. "And how exactly would he do that?"

Paige's mouth trembled. "The Moonlight Strangler is coming after Matthew and you…tonight."

Chapter Two

Paige stood there and waited for Jax to react to the news she'd just delivered.

And he reacted all right.

He turned, ready to bolt inside the house. To protect Matthew, no doubt. But Paige took hold of his arm to stop him.

"Just listen to what I have to say," she insisted. "I don't want to give the Moonlight Strangler a reason to fire shots into the house."

He slung off her grip. "Neither do I, but I'm not going to stand here while he goes after my son."

Our son, she nearly corrected, but Paige figured that was a different battle for a different time. They had to survive this one first.

"The killer likely knows I'm here," she explained, hoping it would get Jax to stay put. "I figure he's watching me. Somehow. Maybe with cameras. Maybe he's out there somewhere in the woods with infrared equipment. He's been watching me for the past three days, though I haven't spotted him yet."

Jax's eyes narrowed. "And even though you knew he was watching, you brought him here, to my doorstep?"

She had no trouble hearing the anger in his voice. Or seeing it on his face. "I didn't have a choice."

"There's always a choice," he snapped.

They weren't just talking about her being here now, but all the other things that'd happened between them. Again, another battle, another time.

Paige stopped him again when he tried to bolt. "The killer would have come here no matter what I did because he knew he'd be able to use Matthew and you to get to me."

He went still. Not in a good way. But in that calm, almost lethal way of a lawman who'd just heard something he didn't want to hear. "And how the heck do you know that?"

"Because he's sent me several texts. And, yes, I'm certain they're from the Moonlight Strangler because he knew details about my attack that hadn't been released to the press. In the last one he sent, he said if I didn't meet him tonight at 9:00 p.m., then he'd go after Matthew and you."

That was still nearly two hours away.

Not much time to pull off a miracle. But it might be enough time to bring all of this to an end. An end that would keep Matthew and Jax out of danger.

Jax stood there, obviously processing that, and cursed again. Glared at her, too.

She deserved the profanity and the glare. Deserved every drop of rage that he wanted to sling at her. Because he was right. She had turned his life upside down. Her precious little boy's, too.

"If you knew the killer was watching you, following you, then why hide here?" Jax asked.

She'd known that question was coming. Others would, too. "Because I didn't want to pull Belinda or your ranch hands into this. I'm not hiding from the killer. I'm hiding from them. That's why I parked by the creek and walked here."

Paige was thankful no one on the ranch had spotted her. Even though she'd altered her appearance, someone could have recognized her. Especially Belinda. They'd known each other since childhood, and a change of hairstyle wasn't going to fool anyone for long.

"At the time I faked my death," she continued, "I thought I was doing the right thing. I thought I was trusting the right people."

"You mean Cord," he snarled.

Paige hated that Jax was aiming his venom at Cord. Because Cord was the one person she was certain had kept his promise to make sure Jax and Matthew stayed out of harm's way.

But someone else had betrayed her.

Paige hoped she got a chance to discover who'd done that and deliver some payback. First, though, she had to protect Matthew—and Jax if he'd let her.

"After the attack, I went to a safe house in the Panhandle," she said. "Not an official safe house," Paige corrected, "but it was a place for me to recover and get back on my feet. Then, I moved to an apartment in Houston. That's where I've been, where I probably would have stayed, if I hadn't started getting those texts from the Moonlight Strangler three days ago."

"And those texts just appeared without any kind of warning or sign that the killer knew you were alive?" His voice stayed a snarl.

"Yes. I'm still trying to figure out how he learned that." She gave a heavy sigh. "Look, I know you have a lot of questions, but they have to wait. We have to put Matthew's safety first."

He couldn't argue with that, but mercy, she was dreading those questions. Dreading even more that she didn't have the answers that Jax wanted to hear.

Jax cursed again before he glanced around the garage, the yard and the back of the house. "I don't want you inside. I don't want Matthew seeing you yet."

"Agreed." Though it broke her heart to say that.

Jax's eyebrow lifted, and he got that look, the one that condemned her as a mother.

"I want to see him and hold him more than I want my next breath," Paige clarified. "But if I go inside, it might give the killer a reason to try to get in there, too. He warned me not to try to hide behind my son."

As if she'd do that.

But she would have to draw Jax into the middle of this. Paige couldn't see a way around it.

"If I'd thought I could make Matthew safer by going inside with him, I would have already been in there," Paige added.

That stirred Jax's jaw muscles, but thankfully he didn't try to bolt toward the house again. However, he did take out his phone, and he moved into the shadows of the garage, his attention nailed to the house.

"I'm texting Belinda to tell her to lock the doors and set the security system," Jax relayed to her. "I'll tell her it's just a precaution, that a prisoner has escaped. And then I'm calling for backup."

Paige didn't stop him from sending the first text. She wanted the house locked down. But she did stop him from texting his brother Jericho. Jericho was the sheriff, and while he would ultimately get involved in this, now wasn't the time. Ditto for Jax's other two brothers, Chase and Levi. They were both lawmen, too, and having them here could make a bad situation worse.

"Hear me out before you involve your brothers in this," she said. "After I got those messages from the Moonlight Strangler, I knew he wasn't going to back down until he had me. I'm the one who got away, and he wants me dead."

"I'm listening," Jax said when she hesitated.

Paige hadn't hesitated because she thought he wasn't listening, but rather because she wasn't sure how to say this. Best just to get it out there. "If I'd thought it would keep Matthew out of danger, I would have just surrendered to him. Would have let him finish what he started."

Jax cursed again. "Do you hear yourself? You're talking about suicide. What you should have done is gone to the cops. Or to me."

"I did come to you, tonight," she whispered. "You won't be thanking me for that, though, but it was the only way. I want this monster dead, and I want you to kill him for me."

He gave a crisp nod. "Tell me where he is, and I will," Jax said as if it were a done deal.

It was far from being a done deal, though.

"He wants me to meet him tonight at nine on the bridge at Appaloosa Creek. I'm sure he already had the area under some kind of surveillance before he told me it was the meeting place. He said if I show up with anyone but you, then he'll start a killing spree. One that will involve *our* son."

She gave him a moment to let that sink in. It didn't sink in well. The fire went through his already fiery blue eyes. Actually, plenty of things about Jax fell into the fiery category. All cowboy, even with that badge clipped to his belt. *Hot* cowboy, she mentally corrected.

Even now, after all this time and water under the bridge, Paige was still attracted to him. Something she shouldn't be remembering. Not when she had more important things to deal with.

"That's why you can't involve your brothers," she added. "If they go rushing to the area, he'll know."

"How?" he snapped.

"I'm not sure. Like I said, I suspect long-range cameras. Of course, that means he has the resources to set up something like that without being detected."

His stare drilled into her. "Who is he?"

A heavy sigh left her mouth. "I honestly don't know."

No one did. The Moonlight Strangler had murdered more than a dozen women before he'd finally made a mistake and left his DNA at a crime scene. There'd been no match for the DNA in the system, but there had been a match of a different kind.

To Jax's adopted sister, Addie.

"As you know, Addie doesn't remember her father," Paige said.

Of course, Addie had been just three when she'd been found wandering around the woods near the Crocketts' Appaloosa Pass Ranch. When no one had come forward to claim her, Jax's parents had adopted her and raised her as their own along with their four sons: Jax, Jericho, Chase and Levi.

"As fraternal twins, Cord was the same age as Addie when he was abandoned, and he doesn't remember anything, either," she went on.

Something Paige had in common with Addie and Cord since she, too, had been left at the hospital when she was a baby. Of course, she hadn't been abandoned by a serial killer.

He got quiet again, but not for long. "Did you see the Moonlight Strangler's face when he tried to kill you?" Jax asked.

This was one of the other questions she'd expected, but Paige had to shake her head and hope she could say the words without having flashbacks or a panic attack.

"He hit me with a stun gun when I was getting into my car in the parking lot of the CSI office in San Antonio," she said. Her words rushed together, spilling out with her breath. "He was wearing a mask so I never saw his face. He said some things to me…cut me and strangled me until I lost consciousness."

Jax pressed his lips together for a moment. "What things did he say?"

That required her to take a moment. Things that were hard to repeat aloud, though they repeated in her head all the time.

And in her nightmares.

"He said if he hadn't managed to get to me, then he would have kidnapped Matthew to draw me out." There. That was the worst of it. The absolute worst. "The next thing I remember after that was waking up with a San Antonio cop leaning over me."

"The cop who helped you fake your death," he mumbled. "Along with Cord." Jax took the venom in his voice up a notch.

Probably because Cord was obsessed with finding and stopping the Moonlight Strangler. But Paige thought maybe she heard something else in Jax's voice. Perhaps a little jealousy. She recognized it because she felt that same ugly emotion when Jax said Belinda's name.

"It's not like that between Cord and me," she volunteered.

His glare didn't soften any. "Then how is it exactly? Why don't you tell me?"

Well, this was a can of worms that she'd hoped to delay opening. The emotions of it were still too raw, and Paige wasn't sure she could tell him without choking on the words. But Jax had to know. Because it was hearing this that would hopefully get him to cooperate with her dangerous plan.

"When the killer was strangling me," she said, but then had to stop to fight back the images of that nightmare. Always the images. "He told me my birth mother was one of his first victims and that he was killing me to make sure her *spawn* didn't live another second."

Judging from the way his eyes widened, Jax hadn't expected that. "And you believed him?"

"No. But the DNA test I took later proved otherwise." That required another deep breath. "According to the test, my birth mother was Mary Madison. Her body was found just a few days after I was abandoned in the hospital. I didn't learn any of this until after I'd faked my death."

"His victim's daughter," Jax said. He did some deep breathing, too, and she could almost see the wheels turning in his head. "That's why he came after you?" But he didn't wait for her to answer. "Then why hasn't he gone after the children of his other victims?"

She had to shake her head. "Maybe my birth mother's murder was more personal to him? Or he could believe I know something about him that the others don't."

"Do you?" he asked, and it sounded like some kind of accusation.

With good reason.

Cord wasn't the only one who'd become obsessed with finding the Moonlight Strangler. She had as well, and even though Paige had dismissed it as part of her job as a crime scene investigator, it'd been more than that. She'd felt it bone deep.

And she'd been right.

She wasn't just searching for a killer who had eluded the cops for nearly thirty years. Now she knew that she'd been looking for the man who'd murdered her mother so she could stop him from killing again. Of course, the obsession had come back to haunt her and just might cost her everything.

"I don't know anything about his identity," she continued, "but I do know how to stop him."

However, it would cost her big-time. The trick was not to have that cost spread to Matthew and Jax.

Paige checked the time. The minutes were ticking away. "I heard you tell Belinda that you were going to the sheriff's office, so she'll be expecting you to leave soon. I suspect you were going to analyze the voice mail I left you."

Jax nodded. "I thought maybe it was a hoax."

Of course he had. Because he hadn't thought she was capable of doing something like faking her own death. "I left the message because I thought it would lessen the blow of you seeing me."

He looked her straight in the eyes. "Nothing could have done that."

True. But she'd had to try. Just as she had to try now.

"So, your plan is to…what?" he asked. "Go to the Appaloosa Creek Bridge and meet a killer who's hellbent on finishing you off?"

Hearing it spelled out like that didn't help, but Paige

tried to push her fear aside. "I'm sure he'd like to finish you off, too. I can't think of another reason he would say I could bring you along."

Jax stayed quiet a moment. "But you're thinking I can kill him before he can get to me?"

Bingo.

He gave her a flat stare. "Of course, the only way I'd get a chance to do that is for him to get close enough to murder you."

Yes. There was no way around that.

"He's never shot anyone before." Not that Paige knew of, anyway. "He'll want an up-close-and-personal kill, like the others." Something that tightened the knot in her stomach. A knot that'd been there for nearly a year since the Moonlight Strangler attacked her.

Jax's next round of profanity was even worse than the others. Before he could tell her a flat-out no, that there was no chance this was going to happen, Paige interrupted him.

"If I could think of another way out, one that didn't involve you, I'd take it. But I can't risk him coming after Matthew. And neither can you."

Jax didn't agree with that. Didn't argue, either.

"He said we're to leave our guns by the side of the road before we approach the bridge," Paige explained. "He has to know that you'll be carrying some kind of backup weapon. That's why I believe he'll use a thermal scan."

"He wouldn't be able to see a gun on thermal scan."

Jax closed his eyes for a second, shook his head. "But he would be able to see the outline of one."

"That's why it can't look like something he'd recognize as a weapon." She took the plastic syringe from her pocket. "Hopefully, it'll look like an ink pen, but it's filled with enough sodium thiopental to incapacitate him in less than thirty seconds."

"Sodium thiopental," he repeated, no doubt knowing that it was a powerful drug that would stop the Moonlight Strangler from moving. It could also kill him, since it was the same drug used in lethal injections for those on death row.

"I would just try to use it on him myself," Paige added, "but he left specific instructions that'll prevent me from doing that."

She took her phone from her jeans pocket and handed it to Jax so he could read the text message for himself. Everything was there. The time and place of the meeting. The offer for her to have Jax and no one else to drive her. If anyone else did show up, the meeting was off, and Jax's house would be attacked. There was also the demand for them to leave their weapons on the side of the road twenty yards from the bridge and then walk there.

And one final demand.

"He wants you to strip down to your underwear so he can make sure you don't have a weapon," Jax read.

She nodded. "Obviously, he doesn't trust me."

"He won't trust me, either," Jax reminded her just as quickly.

"No. He might even have a hired thug hiding nearby to try to take you out. That's why you'll need to wear Kevlar. Do you still keep a vest in your truck?"

Jax nodded. "Kevlar won't stop him from killing you, though."

"No, but it'll stop him from killing you. We can take other precautions for me, like using our own thermal scan of the area." She tipped her head to the small equipment bag she'd stashed behind the truck. "There's a handheld one in there so we can see if anyone's lurking nearby before we surrender our guns."

And there it was. All spelled out for him. Paige just waited to see what he was going to do. Part of her wanted him to refuse. That way, he'd be safe.

For tonight, anyway.

But she didn't believe the killer was bluffing. If he couldn't have her, then he would come after Matthew and Jax and make her suffer a million times more than she would with just her own murder.

Jax looked up at the ceiling as if asking for some divine advice. They needed it. But when his gaze came back to her, he handed Paige her phone and took out his own. He fired off a text and within just a matter of seconds, he got an answer.

"Jericho will be here in five minutes to guard Matthew," he relayed to her.

Jericho's house was less than half a mile away, and she'd hoped he would be able to come right away. Not to try to talk them out of this plan but to help in a way that wouldn't spur an attack at the ranch. Even though

Jericho wouldn't be happy to see her, he would do everything humanly possible to protect Matthew. Not just tonight. But forever.

Good thing, too.

This could be the worst mistake of her life. The worst mistake of Jax's life, too. Because this meeting could make their son an orphan.

"Unless we kill the Moonlight Strangler tonight, you'll have to make sure everything here is secure, that he can't get to Matthew," she reminded him.

Of course, they couldn't shut their little boy away for the rest of his life, and that meant one way or another, someone would have to stop the killer.

"Does Cord know about this plan?" Jax asked.

Paige nodded. "He's in one of the trees across the road with a long-range rifle. He's Jericho's backup. He would have gone with me to the bridge, but the Moonlight Strangler said I could only bring you. Anyone else, and Matthew could be hurt."

Jax's teeth came together. "That's not going to happen."

It was the exact reassurance she needed. One that only a father could give. Yes, Cord would fight to the death for her, but Jax would fight to stay alive so he could keep their son safe.

"Once Jericho is here, we'll come up with some additional security measures," Jax insisted. "He might be able to get a deputy to pose as a hunter so we can scan the woods around the creek before we even get there. That way, we'd still be here if he's detected."

It was a risk, but everything was at this point.

"I saw him," she said, her voice cracking on the last word.

Jax's gaze slashed back to hers. "The killer?"

"Matthew. Belinda had him on the back porch earlier." Mercy, just the memory of seeing him nearly brought her to her knees. "They were on the porch swing, and she was reading to him. He's gotten so big."

No longer a baby. He was a toddler now, almost two years old. Walking and talking. Every second seeing him was like a precious gift that Paige had never thought she'd get.

"I've missed so much." She hadn't meant to say that last part aloud, and it caused Jax to mumble something. She didn't catch exactly what he said, but it was clear he believed that "dying" had been a choice she'd made.

It was.

And at the time it had been her only choice.

She saw the slash of headlights coming toward the garage. Jericho, no doubt. But just in case it wasn't, Paige drew her gun from the back waist of her jeans.

A gesture that had Jax doing the same, along with raising an eyebrow.

Paige had never been much for guns, especially after witnessing her adoptive parents' murders when she was just sixteen. The result of a botched robbery attempt. Since then, guns had always made her squeamish.

"You know how to use that?" Jax asked.

She was about to assure him that she'd learned, but

her phone dinged, and Paige saw the text from the unknown sender.

"It's from the killer," she said. Paige's heart went to her knees when she glanced through the message.

"'Change of plans,'" she read aloud. "'You and Jax start walking to the end of the road *now*. If you bring anyone with you or don't follow the rules, I'll start shooting. The first bullet will go into the house, and I'll aim it right at your son.'"

Chapter Three

Jax's mind was already spinning. He'd been hit with way too much tonight, but all of those whirlwind thoughts flew right out of his head. He pinpointed his focus on the one place it should be.

His son.

His first instinct was to run into the house and hide Matthew and Belinda, but that could turn out to be a fatal mistake. The killer might see it as a violation of his demand and start firing. If the killer was close enough to be capable of doing that.

Jax just didn't know.

And it was too risky to find out.

"Oh, God," Paige mumbled, and she repeated it several times. "We don't have everything in place yet."

No, and Jax figured that was part of the killer's plan. To keep one step ahead of them; to keep them off balance. But Jax didn't intend to let this snake hurt his little boy.

"Text him back," Jax instructed. "Tell him we need more time and that we want the meeting place moved back to the bridge."

It was a long shot. Really long. And a moment later he realized it was no shot at all. "He's blocked me," Paige said.

Of course he had. The killer had delivered his orders, and he wouldn't have them challenged, because he would have almost certainly known that they'd try to negotiate with him.

Jax sent a text of his own. To Belinda. It would terrify her, but again there wasn't much of a choice. He instructed her to take Matthew into the main bathroom and get in the tub. The room was at the center of the house and would be the safest place for them to wait this out. Jax added that he would explain everything later and hoped he was around to do just that.

"Okay, what's wrong?" he heard Jericho ask before his brother even reached the door to the garage.

"I don't have time to get into a lot of details," Jax said, motioning for him to come inside. "Paige is alive, and the Moonlight Strangler is possibly nearby, ready to attack."

Jericho came in, put his hands on his hips, his gaze volleying from Jax to Paige. Jax could tell his brother had plenty of questions, but he also saw the moment when Jericho pushed all those questions aside and the sheriff part of him kicked in.

"What do you need me to do?" Jericho asked.

Jax wasn't sure just yet, but he soon would be. He looked at Paige. "Where's Cord exactly?"

She pointed to a cluster of trees across the road and on the far right side of one of the pastures.

"Text him," Jax ordered her again. "Let him know what's going on and ask if he can see anyone approaching the house."

While she did that, Jax went to her equipment bag and took out the thermal scanner and handed it to Jericho. "I don't know the range on this thing, but I need you to try to see if we're about to be ambushed. Also, call the others for backup."

By others, he meant their brothers, Levi and Chase. Both were lawmen with lots of experience.

Jax also considered having Addie's husband, Weston, come down, but Jax didn't want to leave his sister alone. They had a baby and would be in a very vulnerable position if the Moonlight Strangler wanted to make Addie a target instead of Paige. It'd be a first, since the serial killer had never gone after Addie, but it was too big of a risk to take.

"Cord doesn't see anyone other than us and the ranch hands near the house," Paige relayed to them after reading the response she'd gotten from him. "He wants to know if you trust all your ranch hands."

Jax nearly snapped at that since he didn't like an outsider like Cord questioning men he'd known all his life. But Cord didn't know them, and it was exactly the kind of question a good lawman should ask.

"I trust them," Jax assured her. "Tell him to text us if he sees anyone or anything out of the ordinary."

While she did that, Jericho stayed just inside the doorway, out of range so he wouldn't be seen, and he started up the scanner.

"The Moonlight Strangler wants Paige and me to walk to the end of the road," Jax explained to his brother. He went to his truck and took out the Kevlar vest, tried to hand it to Paige, but she shook her head.

"He'll still want me to strip down," she argued, "so he can make sure I don't have any weapons. And because it's a way of humiliating me. He might let you keep on your clothes, though, because he doesn't plan to let you get close enough to him to use a gun or anything else. That's why the vest is better on you. Put the syringe in your pocket so you can easily get to it. When he's attacking me, you go after him."

Jericho glanced at them as if they'd lost their minds. "Let me see if I'm understanding this. You two are going out there, with a serial killer? One who's already killed Paige once. Or rather, nearly killed her. And she's going to let him attack her again?"

"We don't have a choice," Jax assured him.

Well, maybe they didn't.

The situation was moving so fast that it was hard to think, but Jax didn't need a totally clear head to know that this could turn out to be a huge mistake—no matter what they did.

"Do you see anything on the scanner?" he asked his brother.

Jericho shook his head. "I don't even see Cord."

"He's wearing some kind of thermal blanket," Paige explained. "The kind hunters use. It'll make it harder to be seen on infrared."

That meant the killer and/or his henchmen could

have done the same thing. And probably had. After all, this killer had gotten away with murder for years, so he wasn't an idiot.

But what was he exactly?

Deranged? Obsessed? Or was this more personal for him?

Then it hit him. The Moonlight Strangler had gone after Paige because he considered her a *spawn* of his victim and believed she didn't deserve to live. The killer probably wouldn't want the victim's grandson to live, either. It sickened Jax to think his little boy had any connection to something like that.

"I guess I also don't want to know why Cord was in on this little plan and I wasn't?" Jericho asked.

"Jax didn't know about the plan until a few minutes ago," Paige informed him.

"And yet you're still going along with it," Jericho mumbled. "Yeah, nothing could go wrong with trusting your ex-wife who let you believe she was dead."

Jax ignored his brother's sarcasm and double-checked the Glock in the back waist of his jeans. It'd likely be detected right away, but he might get lucky and be able to keep it.

"You see anyone?" Jax asked him.

"No. But like you said, we don't know the range on this thing. Somebody could still be out there, hiding under a thermal wrap. Somebody who'll kill you. That vest isn't going to protect you from a head shot."

Nor a shot that would incapacitate him in some other

way. "I don't think he wants to kill me. Just Paige. And he doesn't want to put a bullet in her."

Damn, that sounded ice-cold. But it was the truth. The Moonlight Strangler would want his hands on her.

Paige went closer to his brother. She was ash pale now, and her hands were trembling. "I know you don't owe me any favors, Jericho, but if something goes wrong, stay here to protect Matthew."

Jericho doled out a glare to her as if he might confirm the no-favors part, but he nodded. "I'll protect him."

Jax knew his brother would. And Jax would do the same for him. "When Levi and Chase get here, tell them what's going on. Don't have them follow us, but if they can position themselves in front of the house and closer to the road, they might be able to give us some backup."

"Cord might be able to do that, too," Paige added. "He's got sniper training."

Good. Jax would take anything he could get at this point, but he really didn't want bullets flying near the house. Too bad he couldn't guarantee that wouldn't happen, and that meant Paige and he needed to put as much distance between them and the house as possible.

"We need to leave now," Paige pressed, already starting out of the garage.

Jax knew she was right, but he still took a moment to look around, to see if there was anything he could do to make this plan safer.

There wasn't.

He could see more headlights coming from the road that led to the main ranch and to his brothers' houses. Chase and Levi, no doubt. Jericho would have to explain to them what was happening and get in the best positions to protect Matthew.

In the meantime, all Jax could do was get moving toward this showdown with a killer.

Since there was no truly safe position for Paige, Jax fell into step beside her. However, he did maneuver her to his right.

"If someone fires shots, drop down into the ditch," he instructed, pointing at the ground. It wouldn't be ideal protection since it was only a few feet deep, but it was better than nothing.

He glanced back at the house to make sure Belinda wasn't at the window. She wasn't. Hopefully, she would stay put with Matthew in the bathroom until she got the okay from him.

Hell.

He hated putting his son through this. Matthew was too young to understand the danger, but he had to sense something was wrong. After all, he should be getting dinner about now, followed by reading time with his daddy. He shouldn't have to be holed up in a bathtub, hiding from a serial killer.

"I'm so sorry," Paige whispered.

"Don't," Jax warned her. Any apology she attempted would be useless right now and might mess with his head. "And keep watch."

Of course, she was already doing that. Her gaze was

firing all around them. Jax couldn't be sure, but he thought he heard her mumble a prayer. Good. Because he was certainly saying a few of them, too.

Paige took out her phone, checked the screen. No doubt for an update from Cord or the killer. But there was nothing on the screen. Ditto for his own phone. No word yet from his brothers. Jax decided to believe that was good news, because if they'd spotted someone in the area, Jericho would have certainly let him know about it.

The road wasn't long, less than a quarter of a mile from his house to the highway that led into town. It wasn't a straight shot, though. It'd once been an old ranch trail, and it coiled around massive oaks and other trees that dotted the acres of land. Those deep curves in the road would no doubt prevent Cord or his brothers from being able to see what was going on.

There were no lights out here, but it wasn't pitch dark yet. Soon would be, though.

And there was a moon.

Since the killer had struck only on nights with a visible moon and left the crescent shaped cuts on his victims' cheeks, that's how he'd earned his nickname. Maybe he wouldn't add another victim or two to his list tonight.

"Still no text from him," Paige mumbled, checking her phone again.

No text from his brothers, either, but Jax did spot something. So did Paige because she stopped, and they both stared at the truck ahead. It was parked right where the ranch road met the highway. The lights were off, and it was positioned so that it blocked any vehicle from getting on or off the ranch. Unfortunately, this made it impossible for Jax to read the license plates, although they were probably stolen, anyway.

"You see anyone inside?" Paige asked.

Jax had to shake his head. Too dark, and the windows had a dark tint, too. He fired off a text to Jericho. Try to use the scanner. You might not be able to see it, but there's a truck parked at the end of the road.

Then he turned to Paige to tell her to text Cord and ask him to do the same thing, but Paige was already in the process of taking care of that.

Nothing, Jericho texted back. I got a glimpse of the truck through the trees, but it's too far away for the scanner.

Yeah, that's what Jax figured, and he also figured that's why the killer had parked it in that particular location.

"Cord's not getting anything on his scanner," Paige relayed to Jax when she got a response. "He's too far away to see the truck and is going to try to move closer. He'll be careful," she added.

No doubt. But careful might not be nearly good enough.

Jax didn't draw his gun, but he kept his hand over it, and he started toward the truck again. Still no sign of anyone inside, and Paige and he were still a good fifteen yards away when her phone dinged with a text message.

Not Cord this time.

"It's from the killer," she said, showing him the screen. "'Guns down on the ground,'" she read aloud. "'Paige, you know what to do.'"

That was it, all the instruction they were going to get, but Paige did indeed know what to do. She shucked off her top, dropping it on the ground next to where Jax placed his Glock. He kept the backup gun in the back of his jeans.

Her shoes and jeans came off next, along with her gun.

"Sorry," she repeated.

It took Jax a moment to realize the apology was aimed at him. And another moment to realize why. That's because he was gawking at her in her bra and panties, and she was apologizing for putting him in this awkward situation.

Talk about bad timing, but Paige always had grabbed his attention. A half-naked Paige could grab it even more.

"He must be somewhere in or around the truck," Paige said. She took a deep breath, then another, and started walking.

Jax could only imagine what was going through her head right now. The Moonlight Strangler had nearly killed her, but here she was, ready to face him head-on.

Part of him admired that, especially since she was doing this to save Matthew. But another part of him remembered how they'd gotten to this point in the first place. She'd become the killer's target because she was obsessed with finding him.

As a lawman, it was hard for him to fault her for that.

As a father, he hated that she'd put Matthew on this monster's radar.

Her phone dinged, and she held it up for Jax to see. Good girl, the killer taunted. Put your hands on top of your head and keep walking. Deputy Crockett, you stop where you are. Don't make any sudden moves, or I'll put bullets in both of you. And if you've got a gun hidden away, the best way to get Paige killed would be to try to use that gun on me.

Not good. They were still five yards away. Not nearly close enough for him to lunge at a killer.

"Why don't you come out so we can talk face-to-face?" Jax called out. He didn't expect a response.

That's why he was shocked when he got one.

"Talking won't help," a man said. Jax didn't recognize his voice because he was using a scrambler device. Didn't see him, either. "Paige, turn around a sec so I can make sure you don't have a gun tucked in those panties. Nice color, by the way. Would you call that pink or peach?"

This wasn't just a killer, but a sick one.

"Pink," she said through clenched teeth when she finished circling around.

"Nice. Now, do what you know you have to do."

She looked at Jax, their gazes holding, and even in the darkness he had no trouble seeing the fear.

And her surrender.

"Just make sure you kill him," she whispered. "He can't walk out of here alive."

Yes, because he would try to hurt Matthew. Jax knew what he had to do.

Paige took another step toward the truck.

"I told you to stay put, Deputy," the man warned him when Jax moved, too. "I want you to watch."

Definitely not good.

That's the reason the killer had allowed him out here, just so he could witness Paige's murder. Jax had to do something, and he had to do it fast.

"I want to tell Paige goodbye," Jax said.

Paige froze, glanced back at him, no doubt questioning what the heck he was doing. What he was doing was trying to bargain with this fool. Or maybe distract him. Anything that would prevent him from getting his hands on Paige again.

With that stunned look still on her face, Jax went to her, positioning himself between the truck and her, and he pulled her into his arms. She was board-stiff and trembling, but that didn't stop Jax from dropping a kiss on her mouth.

While he slipped the syringe into the elastic of her panties. He made sure the protective plastic cap was secure enough so that she wouldn't accidentally stab herself with it.

"I'll get to you as fast as I can," Jax whispered in her ear, hoping it was a promise he could keep.

Paige nodded. Started walking away.

But she'd barely made it a step when Jax heard the rustling sounds to his right.

And to his left.

The dark shadowy figures were wearing ski masks, and they came out of the ditches, fast, barreling right at them. Jax didn't even have time to react. One of them plowed right into him and knocked him to the ground.

Before he could even grab his backup weapon, the man put a gun to Jax's head.

Chapter Four

From the corner of her eye, Paige saw the man go right at Jax.

She screamed for him to look out, or rather that's what she tried to do, but the sound didn't quite make it to her throat. That's because the hulking man crashed right into her, throwing her to the ground and knocking the breath right out of her.

The pain burst through her.

The fear and dread, too.

She'd failed, and these two goons would almost certainly try to kill Jax and her. Was one of them the Moonlight Strangler? Or were these just his henchmen? If so, they would no doubt deliver them to the Moonlight Strangler so he could finish them off and then go after Matthew.

That couldn't happen.

Even though she was fighting to regain her breath, Paige slammed her elbow into the man's stomach. It felt as if she'd hit a brick wall. He didn't even react to the blow, but he did latch on to her hair and yank her to a standing position with her back against his chest. He put a gun to her head.

And that's when she got a good look at Jax.

Her heart went to her knees. No! Jax was being held at gunpoint, too. She'd prayed that he had managed to get away, but like her he was now a captive.

"Move and your ex dies," the man growled in her ear.

That stopped her, but then Paige realized the other goon had likely told Jax the same thing because Jax wasn't fighting. He was looking at her and shaking his head, no doubt trying to remind her not to do anything stupid. Of course, she'd already done something stupid by allowing the danger to get this close to Matthew and him.

"I'm sorry," she mouthed.

However, that only earned her another one of Jax's glares.

"What now?" Jax asked, and it took her a moment to realize he wasn't talking to her but rather to the thug who had his arm hooked around his neck.

Neither of the men jumped to answer, but Paige did hear some chatter. She glanced back and saw that it was coming through a tiny communicator fitted into the man's ear. No doubt the voice of the Moonlight Strangler, and he was almost certainly doling out instructions.

Instructions on how he wanted them murdered.

She'd been a fool to think she could outsmart him. A fool to involve Jax in this. She should have just come to the meeting alone. Yes, the Moonlight Strangler would have just finished what he'd started all those months ago, but at least Jax would be inside his house where he could hopefully be protecting Matthew.

The chattering sound stopped, but Paige heard something else. Movement to her right, in the direction of the Crockett ranch. Maybe Jericho or Cord. Unfortunately, the hired thug must have heard it, too, because he dragged her back to the ground. Across from her, the guy holding Jax did the same to him.

The road was still hot, though the sun had already set, and the small rocks and debris dug into her skin. So did the syringe. It hadn't cracked when she fell, thank God, but she might have a hard time getting to it now that the goon had her on her stomach. However, she had managed to keep hold of her phone, and while it wasn't an ideal weapon, she might be able to bash him with it.

"Come any closer, and they both get bullets to the heads," the brute holding her called out when she heard the sound of more movement.

She doubted Jericho or Cord would just come charging in there, but maybe one or both of them could get into a position to have a clean shot.

More chatter came from the earpiece, and this time Paige caught three words. Her own name and a simple sentence that chilled her from head to toe.

She's mine.

Paige knew exactly what he meant by that. He wanted to do the job himself.

"Shoot the deputy if anyone fires at us or tries to come closer," the hired gun told his comrade. "Hear that?" he said in a much louder voice, no doubt to Cord, Jericho or whoever else was approaching. "Jax Crockett pays the price if you try to save her."

The man hauled her back to her feet, and he shoved the gun even harder against her temple. Even in the darkness, Paige managed to make eye contact with Jax. *Brief* eye contact. Enough for her to see his gaze drop to her panties. Or rather to the syringe he'd put there.

"Use it," Jax mouthed. Even though he didn't make any sound when he spoke, his captor must have realized Jax was trying to communicate with her because he tightened the chokehold on Jax.

Paige wasn't even sure she could get the syringe without either of them getting shot, but she had to try. And she didn't have much time, either. The man started moving her toward the truck. Once he had her inside the vehicle, there wouldn't be any reason for them to keep Jax alive. Probably the only reason they hadn't already killed him was to get her to cooperate.

And that's what Paige did—she cooperated.

Or rather that's what she pretended to do. She let the man maneuver her away from Jax, and she looked for her chance to make a move. That chance came when she spotted a rock on the road. It wasn't big, but when they reached it, Paige stumbled, pretending to trip.

She would have fallen if the man hadn't yanked her back by her hair. That hurt, but it was a drop in the bucket compared to the pain that exploded through her head when the man bashed the butt of his gun against her temple.

Paige dropped down again, but there was no faking it this time.

Mercy. She was able to choke back a scream but couldn't stop the groan of pain that tore from her throat.

Jax must have heard the groan because he shouted something. Something she didn't catch because both her head and ears were throbbing. She couldn't hear much of anything, but thankfully her hands worked just fine.

Fueled with the anger from the attack and the fear that Jax would get killed trying to save her, Paige yanked out the syringe and used her thumb to flick off the plastic tip from the needle. In the same motion, she stood, spun around and jammed the syringe right into the man's neck.

The shot blasted through the air. And it took her a moment to realize he hadn't shot her. He'd pulled the trigger all right, but his shot had slammed into the road. Thank God. She didn't want any bullets going anywhere in the direction of the house.

The thug staggered back, reaching for her, but Paige shoved him to the ground. Too bad the drug didn't immediately cause him to lose consciousness, because he tried once again to shoot her. However, Paige grabbed his wrist and held on.

"Paige!" Jax shouted.

She wasn't sure exactly where he was or what he wanted her to do, and Paige didn't have time to find out. The man tried to take aim at her, and even though his hands were as wobbly as the rest of him, she didn't want him to get off another shot. They might not be so lucky this time.

The man cursed her, his words slurred, and his head dropped back a little. Paige took advantage of that and used his own gun to knock him in the head. When that didn't work, she hit him again. And again. Finally, he slumped to the ground, his eyes closing and his body going limp.

One down, at least two to go.

Paige snatched up the gun and glanced in the direction of the truck to make sure the Moonlight Strangler or another attacker wasn't taking aim at her. But she saw no one. However, when her gaze slashed toward Jax, she spotted something that put her heart right back in her throat.

Jax, in a fight for his life.

Both Jax and the goon were on the ground, and the goon still had control of the gun. As she had done, Jax was trying to get control while also trying to keep the guy's aim away from the direction of the house.

"Cord, watch the truck," Paige called out, though she was certain that if he was in position, he was already doing that.

Paige didn't waste a second. She ran toward Jax. She didn't want Jax and her to be ambushed while her back was turned, but he was unarmed and outsized. If she didn't help, this could turn even more dangerous than it already was.

Paige was just a few feet away when she heard a sound she didn't want to hear. Another blast. Her stomach and muscles were already in knots, but that tightened her chest so much that she couldn't breathe. Jax couldn't be hurt. He just couldn't be.

And he wasn't.

It took her a moment to fight through the panic, especially when she saw the blood. Thankfully, it wasn't on Jax. It was on the thug, and spreading across the front of his shirt. Now Jax had the man's gun in his own hand.

Jax cursed, moved away from the man, but he didn't lower the gun. He kept it aimed at him while he volleyed glances between the truck, the other man and her.

"You're hurt," Jax said.

Was she? Paige wasn't sure of anything right now except the relief of seeing Jax unharmed.

"Is one of them the Moonlight Strangler?" someone called out.

Cord.

She didn't spot him right away, but Paige followed the sound of his voice. He was in the pasture, moving toward the truck.

Jax spared Cord a glance, too. And a glare. Before he yanked the ski mask off the man he'd just shot. There was just enough light from the silvery moon for her to see his face.

A stranger.

And he wasn't nearly old enough to be the serial killer. The Moonlight Strangler had been murdering women for three decades, and this man appeared to be in his twenties.

He was also dead.

Paige could tell from his now-lifeless eyes, which were fixed in a permanent blank stare.

"Is the other one alive?" Jax asked.

She shook her head. "I'm not sure." Paige looked back at the guy, but he hadn't moved since she'd bashed him with the gun. "But he's got some kind of communicator in his ear. I think he was talking to the Moonlight Strangler."

Jax hurried toward the man but then almost immediately stopped. Paige did, too, when she heard the sound of the footsteps. She got another slam of adrenaline. Followed by relief when she saw that it was Jericho.

Good. Well, maybe.

It was possible the Moonlight Strangler was in that truck and was ready to gun them all down. Of course, Cord was racing toward it no doubt to try to prevent that from happening.

"Call an ambulance," Jax told his brother.

Probably in case the second thug was still alive. But she rethought that when Jericho looked at her and cursed. And when she felt the blood sliding down the side of her head and face. She wiped it away but felt a new trickle follow right behind it.

God knew how bad she looked right now or even how badly she was hurt. Her head and body were throbbing, but Paige wasn't getting in the ambulance. She had to stop the Moonlight Strangler once and for all.

Jax cursed her, too, when he realized she was trailing after him, and he automatically adjusted his position so that he was in between the truck and her. Protecting her. Despite the bad blood between them, that didn't surprise her. It wasn't just the lawman in him that made him do that. Jax had always had this cowboy code about protecting others.

Even if she probably wasn't someone he wanted to protect.

Jax approached the second man with caution. His gun aimed, his gaze still firing all around them. He reached down, pulled off the mask and put his fingers to the man's neck.

"He's alive," Jax relayed. "Barely."

Paige leaned in, hoping this would be the Moonlight Strangler. But he wasn't. Like the other man, he was much too young. And that meant the killer could indeed be in the truck or nearby.

"Be careful," she called out to Cord.

Whether he'd listen was anyone's guess. Unlike Jax, Cord didn't have that whole protection code. He had one goal. Just one.

To catch his biological father, no matter what the cost. That included sacrificing his own life.

Paige had been driven by that kind of justice after her parents had been murdered. That was the reason she'd become a CSI. But justice didn't drive her now. She only wanted to keep Jax and her son safe. That might finally happen if the Moonlight Strangler was in the truck so they could catch him.

But if he was there, why hadn't he driven off when he'd seen that his thugs had failed?

A possible answer popped into her head. An answer she didn't like one bit.

This could be a trap.

Jax must have realized the same thing because his attention went straight to the truck. And to Cord.

"Watch out!" Jax shouted.

However, the words had hardly left his mouth when the blast thundered through the air. And the truck burst into a ball of fire.

Chapter Five

Jax cursed when he read Jericho's latest text message. More bad news. Just what he didn't need right now since he'd already had enough of that tonight.

Both men who'd attacked Paige and him couldn't be interrogated. One had died at the scene from the gunshot wound Jax delivered to the guy's chest. The other one, the man Paige had injected with the syringe, was in the hospital but hadn't regained consciousness. Until he did, he couldn't give Jax answers about the snake who'd hired them.

The only good thing to come out of this was that Matthew was safe and only the one hired gun was dead. Of course, not everyone had come out of it unscathed. He had proof of that right in front of him. Both Cord and Paige were side by side on examining tables in the ER while nurses stitched them up.

Plus, the ER looked like a top-secret facility, what with two security guards standing in the doorway of the room. Anyone coming into the building was being searched for weapons, and everyone was on alert to make sure more hired guns didn't try to come after Paige and him.

"What's wrong?" Paige asked, no doubt because she'd heard his mumbled profanity over the text. No doubt, too, because she was watching him so closely. But then, he was watching her, too.

Paige was alive.

And now that the dust had partially settled from the attack, Jax would need to deal with that. He'd have to deal with a lot of things, and he started with Matthew.

His brothers Chase and Levi were at Jax's house standing guard. The ranch hands were patrolling the grounds and had already searched the perimeter for snipers. Added to that, the road leading to the ranch was a crime scene now and was crawling with Texas Rangers, CSIs, the bomb squad, firefighters and even two of Appaloosa Pass's own reserve deputies. With all those people on the grounds, Jax's house was on lockdown and would stay that way until he could get home and move Matthew to a safer location.

Wherever that would be.

Belinda certainly wanted to know that, too, because she'd called twice and then left a voice mail when Jax hadn't answered her third call. He knew the nanny was worried, as well she should be, but right now he wouldn't be able to do much to calm any of her fears.

Jax walked closer, though he already had Paige's attention. Cord's as well because he ended his latest phone call and stared at Jax.

"There wasn't a body in the truck," Jax explained.

"The bomb guys have cleared the CSI team to go in and start gathering evidence, but the explosive device inside the truck appears to have been on a timer."

Paige released the breath she'd obviously been holding, and despite the fact that she was getting stitches near her hairline, she shook her head. "They didn't find the Moonlight Strangler," she said. Not a question. Probably because she knew Jax wouldn't be scowling if they'd managed to nail the SOB.

"Somebody drove that truck to the ranch," Cord snapped. He had two nurses working on him, and they were stitching up his head, arms and even his left leg. They'd cut his jeans to get to the wound. "That means he escaped."

Jax nodded. Then shrugged. "But we don't know for sure the Moonlight Strangler was even there. Do we?" And he made sure there was displeasure in his tone. Plenty of it. Because Jax was still riled to the core that he hadn't been included in this stupid plan before it'd turned deadly.

"He wants to kill me," Paige stated. "He would have been close enough to make sure he could do that."

No displeasure in her voice, but there was plenty of frustration and pain, both physical and otherwise. She winced when the nurse added another stitch.

"Sorry, Paige," the nurse apologized. She was Misty Carlton, someone Jax and Paige had known their entire lives. Ditto for the other nurses working on Cord. With all the other folks coming in and out of the ER,

Cord figured it was already all over town that Paige was alive.

He'd have to deal with that, too.

The other members of his family would have to be told. And Matthew, of course. His son was too young to remember Paige, but Jax doubted he could keep Paige from Matthew. Well, not forever, anyway. But for now, he pushed that problem aside and went with the most obvious one.

Jax shifted his attention to Cord. "You couldn't talk Paige out of going through with this plan to meet with your birth father?"

Cord's jaw muscles flickered and tensed. No doubt because of the birth father reference. Yeah, it was a petty dig, but Jax was pissed off that a trained DEA agent— supposedly a top-notch one, too—had allowed a victim to arrange a showdown with a serial killer.

"Have you ever been able to talk Paige out of anything?" Cord countered.

That was a petty dig, as well. But it was the truth. To say that Paige was hardheaded was like saying the sky had a little bit of blue in it.

"Don't blame Cord for this," Paige spoke up. "If he hadn't come with me, I would have done it alone."

Jax was certain that tightened some of his own jaw muscles. "Of course you would have, and look where it got you." His gaze went back to Cord. "Have you tried to find a personal link between Paige's biological mother, Mary, and the Moonlight Strangler?" Especially since Mary was one of the Moonlight Strangler's first known victims.

"Of course," Cord snapped, clearly insulted that Jax had asked the obvious. "I haven't found one yet. And yes, I did alert the FBI when Paige's DNA test came back as a match to Mary's."

"Any reason you didn't tell me?" Jax pressed.

"Because I asked him not to," Paige volunteered before Cord could say anything. "I thought if too many people were trying to make the connection between Mary and me that the Moonlight Strangler would suspect I was alive."

Jax was already riled six ways to Sunday, and that didn't help. "I'm not 'too many people.'" He nearly added he was her husband.

But he wasn't. Not anymore.

However, he was still a lawman and the father of her son. That alone should have earned him a place in the inner circle of information.

"The FBI decided to keep it secret, too," Cord went on. "Until they can look for a possible link. The lead investigator said there were already too many hands in this particular case."

No surprise there. The FBI had been keeping lots of things about this close to the vest. Not that it'd helped. The Moonlight Strangler always seemed to be in the know.

Especially when it came to Paige.

Jax was on the verge of questioning her about that, but his phone buzzed before he could say anything. Not

Jericho this time, but it was another family member. Or rather a soon-to-be family member. Levi's fiancée.

"It's Alexa," Jax relayed to Paige.

That didn't help Paige's already pale color, and Jax didn't have to guess why. Alexa Dearborn and Paige had been best friends, and Paige had even worked for Alexa's security company when Alexa had been investigating the Moonlight Strangler. It was Paige's involvement that led to her nearly being killed.

Jax answered the call but didn't put it on speaker. "Is it true?" Alexa asked right off. "Is Paige really alive?"

Even though Paige couldn't have heard her old friend's voice, she no doubt guessed what Alexa had asked. "Tell her I'll call her first chance I get," Paige said.

"She's alive," Jax told the woman. "And she'll call you later."

Silence. For several long moments. Followed by a hoarse sob from Alexa. No doubt a sob of relief. Later, she'd have questions, but for now Alexa was likely glad that the past months had been just a nightmare and that her friend was alive.

Jax ended the call and slipped his phone into his pocket. "Alexa's engaged to Levi now."

More surprise went through her eyes. Then approval. Alexa and Levi had always had a thing for each other, but until recently Levi—and Jax—hadn't been able to get past Alexa's connection to what'd happened to Paige.

Or rather what they had thought had happened to her.

"Alexa's been beating herself up about your 'death.'" Jax hadn't said that to make Paige feel any guiltier about what she'd done.

All right, maybe he had.

Hell. This sliced into him like a knife, and Jax wasn't sure where to aim these old and new feelings. Old because he remembered the obsession that'd torn them apart. An obsession in part because of Alexa's investigation into the Moonlight Strangler.

The old attraction was still there between Paige and him, too. Jax had gotten a reminder of that when she'd stripped down on the road. Thankfully, she was dressed now in the jeans and shirt she'd been wearing when she had first arrived at the ranch.

And she was also sporting that pained look on her face.

That's where the new feelings played into this. He'd never seen Paige afraid and in pain. But she was now.

Their gazes held, and things passed between them. Unspoken things that only former lovers could share.

"I need to see Matthew," Paige said.

Well, that took care of any reminders of the old attraction. "It's not safe."

"Make it safe." Her voice broke. Tears sprang to her eyes. "Please."

Until she'd added that *please* and he'd seen the tears, Jax had been ready to flat-out refuse. He still might. But the trouble was, Paige had a legal right to see their son. Well, unless he could force Paige into protective custody with the marshals. Or he could whisk Matthew away to a safe house out of her reach. Either or both of those things might happen, but Jax was a long way from making that decision.

Since Jax couldn't figure out what to do right now, he turned back to Cord.

But Cord didn't appear to be in a conversing kind of mood. Even though he was still getting stitched up, he stood when his phone rang. He only glanced at the screen but didn't answer the call.

"I have to go," Cord insisted. He looked at Paige and added, "I'll be in touch. And remember, don't do anything stupid."

The nurses and Paige looked at him as if he'd lost his mind. "We're not finished," one of the nurses pointed out, but she was talking to the air because Cord started for the door. He would have just walked out if Jax hadn't stepped in front of him.

"You might want to take this drive for justice down a notch," Jax advised him.

Cord met his gaze head-on with eyes that Jax recognized because they were a genetic copy of Addie. It was strange to see Addie's usually loving eyes stare back at him with this raw intensity.

"My birth father's a serial killer who's targeted your wife," Cord said like a warning. And Jax doubted Cord was stating the obvious to hear himself talk. This was a reminder that Jax had no say in this as far as Cord was concerned.

"Ex-wife," Jax automatically corrected, and hated that it was nitpicking.

Cord continued to stare at him. "He's targeted Paige and God knows who else. I want him stopped."

Jax did his own stating the obvious. "Everyone wants him stopped. But you need to take some precautions. You nearly got yourself killed tonight."

"Nearly is good enough. I'm walking out of here alive, and I *will* find him." With that, Cord pushed past Jax. Past Jericho, too, who was coming in as Cord was going out.

"Mr. Sunshine," Jericho grumbled, upping Cord's scowl with one of his own.

That was a little like the pot calling the kettle black, since Jericho wasn't exactly a cheerful sort of guy. The nurses must have thought so as well because the one working on Paige quickly finished up, and she eased out of the room along with the other two who'd stitched up Cord.

Jericho's attention, however, didn't remain focused on Cord. He turned toward Paige. Or rather glared at her. "Do I want to know why you faked your own death?" Jericho asked.

She took a moment, probably because she needed it. It'd been a helluva long night, and it was just starting. "At the time, I thought it was the only option I had. Don't say I told you so," she added.

Jericho didn't say the words, but his shrug and flat look conveyed it. Jax agreed. Paige had had other options, but she hadn't taken them. She could have let him know she was alive so he could have arranged protective custody for her. For Matthew, too.

"Please tell me you found the Moonlight Strangler," Paige said.

"Afraid not." And Jericho glanced at a note he'd made on his phone. "Do the names Luca Paulino and Brady Loveland mean anything to you?"

Paige repeated them and shook her head. "No. Who are they?"

"They're the men who attacked Jax and you. Paulino's the dead one. Loveland's still out cold. Both had mile-long rap sheets so we were able to match their prints, but neither has an obvious connection to the Moonlight Strangler."

Jax didn't bother to groan, because it was news that he'd expected. The Moonlight Strangler had avoided capture for over thirty years, and he wouldn't have left a paper trail or any loose ends to lead back to him. And Loveland was definitely a loose end.

"You have a guard on Loveland?" Jax asked his brother.

Jericho nodded. "Dexter and Mack."

Both deputies. Good. Because if the Moonlight Strangler tried to silence Loveland forever, then Dexter and Mack would be there to stop him.

"The Moonlight Strangler's never used hired guns before," Paige said. It sounded as if she was thinking aloud.

Both Jericho and Jax made a sound of agreement. This particular serial killer was usually a loner. Yes, he frequently texted, wrote or even called people connected to the investigation, but to the best of Jax's knowledge, tonight was the first time the Moonlight Strangler had hired thugs to help him.

Why?

"He probably knew we wouldn't just hand Paige over without a fight, so he could have come prepared." Jax was thinking out loud, too.

Except he clearly hadn't given it enough thought because he'd made it sound personal. It was, in a way. But Jax wouldn't have handed over anyone to the Moonlight Strangler. Paige included.

"You believe someone else was behind the attack?" Jericho asked, studying him.

"Maybe." The Moonlight Strangler was still his top suspect, but Jax wanted to add another possibility to the list. "Darrin Pittman could have put this plan together."

Jax could tell that Paige was startled just by the mention of the man's name. She opened her mouth and looked ready to dismiss it, but then it must have sunk in that he could be right.

"Pittman," she repeated in a hoarse whisper.

Paige was no doubt reliving a different set of memories. Not as nightmarish as those the Moonlight Strangler had given her, but Pittman hated Paige enough to do something like this.

"That's the rich college football player who accused you of planting false evidence at a crime scene," Jericho said to her.

She nodded. "I gathered his DNA from a rape scene. A frat party gone terribly wrong. He said I put the DNA there. I didn't." Paige pushed her hair from her face and then winced when she brushed her fingers over the stitches. "Anyway, Pittman threatened and harassed me." Her gaze slid to Jax. "Please tell me he was convicted of those rape charges and is in jail."

Jax knew she wasn't going to like his answer. "No. He got off on a legal technicality. Nothing to do with the evidence you gathered, but a goof-up in his interrogation with the cops. He didn't get any jail time, but he lost his scholarship and was kicked out of school."

Paige groaned. "He's dangerous and shouldn't be on the street."

Jax agreed. He wouldn't mention that he'd nearly punched Pittman in the face when he'd shown up at the sheriff's office after Paige's "death" to gloat about Paige "getting what she deserved." Jericho had had to hold Jax back. But even Jax's threats for Pittman to back off hadn't stopped the man. Pittman had continued to demonstrate his hatred for Paige by posting slurs about her on social media.

"And you think he could want Paige dead?" Jericho pressed.

"Oh, yeah. He'd love to see her dead." No doubt about that in Jax's mind. "Pittman sent party balloons to Paige's funeral, and the headstone on her grave's been vandalized a few times. I'm sure he's the one who did it."

Paige shuddered, maybe at the realization of how much Pittman hated her. Maybe at the reminder that she easily could have been in that grave.

"I'll arrange to have Pittman brought in for a little chat," Jericho offered. "Is there any way Pittman could have found out you're alive and orchestrated this botched showdown?"

"No." But she quickly shook her head. "Maybe. If Pittman suspected I was alive, he has the money to have hired plenty of PIs to locate me. But those first three texts I got weren't from him. Pittman couldn't have known those details of my attack. Those were from the Moonlight Strangler, and I'm not sure how he found me. It's possible though Pittman learned through him or through someone else."

"Someone else?" Jericho questioned.

She dodged his gaze. Not a good sign.

"Leland Fountain," she finally said. "He's the sergeant at SAPD who found me after the attack and reported me dead."

"He's the one who helped you fake your death?" Jax cursed. "I know him."

Paige nodded. "Leland and I dated for a while right after high school."

Yeah. Jax didn't need to be reminded of that. Paige and he had broken up for a few months right before she started college, and she'd met Leland. Jax didn't think it'd gotten too serious between Paige and Leland, mainly because she'd come back to Appaloosa Pass and him. But maybe the relationship had been more serious than he'd originally thought.

"And you think Leland could have told Pittman you were alive?" Jericho pressed.

No gaze dodging or hesitation this time. "No. Not intentionally, anyway. But it's possible he let something slip."

Jax thought there was something else she wasn't saying. Something he wasn't going to want to hear, but he didn't get a chance to press her on it because Paige's phone made a dinging sound to indicate she had a text message.

She dug her phone from her pocket, her face bunching up with every little move. Probably because she was sore and bruised from the fall she'd taken during the attack. However, her forehead bunched up even more when she saw the screen.

"Unknown caller." Paige's voice had little sound. "It's from the Moonlight Strangler. He's the only person other than Cord and Leland who sends me messages."

Her gaze skimmed over the screen, and with her hands shaking, she gave the phone to Jax so he could see it for himself. And what he saw was the string of profanity. Really bad curse words. All aimed at Paige. After that was a short warning:

This isn't over.

Jax hadn't thought for one second that it was, but it seemed to shake Paige to the core to see it spelled out like that.

Jericho read through the message, too, and he stared at the phone a moment before looking at Paige. "How do you know this is actually from the Moonlight Strangler?"

The question seemed to throw her for a moment, maybe because she thought Jericho was disputing what she'd told them. "Because the killer's been texting me, and like I told Jax, he knew details about my attack that weren't released to the press. Details that only me, the killer and Leland knew. Pittman certainly didn't know so he couldn't have sent the texts to set this up. Those had to have come from the Moonlight Strangler."

Jericho held up the phone for her to see. "And he used this much name-calling and profanity?"

She studied the message again. "No. He usually just taunts me with that sugary, sick tone. Why? Do you think it means something? Do you think Pittman could have sent this one?"

"Maybe." But Jericho shook his head, groaned. "Then again, the Moonlight Strangler's not exactly predictable. How'd he get your phone number, anyway?"

"I don't know. The account is under the alias I've been using, and I never give out the number. Not even to my doctor. I have a prepaid cell I use for that. I'm guessing the Moonlight Strangler found me somehow and then had someone hack into my computer to get the number from my online account."

It was possible. They didn't know if the Moonlight Strangler had the money and resources to launch a full-scale search, but Jax was betting he did. Plus, that crescent-shaped scar on Paige's face was like a brand. Anyone who saw it might recognize it as the killer's signature, and the Moonlight Strangler had groupies.

One of those sickos could have seen it and then gotten word to the killer.

Jericho's attention shifted to Jax. "When you take Paige's statement, compare this text to the others she's gotten. In fact, have everything on her phone analyzed because we need to know if Pittman has inserted himself into this by sending this latest text."

That was already on Jax's to-do list. A list that had gotten way too long. He needed to get started on whittling it down.

There was a soft knock on the door, and both Jericho and Jax automatically reached for their guns. But it was a false alarm. It was Misty Carlton, the nurse.

Misty sucked in her breath, no doubt alarmed by their reaction, and she lifted her hand to show them some papers. "It's Paige's release forms from the doctor. She can go home now."

Misty's info was simple enough, but Jericho, Paige and he just stood there staring at the nurse.

She can go home now.

Yes, but the question was—would Jax let her?

Paige got up from the examining table and took the papers. "Thank you," she told Misty, and then turned to face Jax. "Please, just let me see Matthew."

Jax considered saying no. After all, he could remind her that it wasn't safe, but the truth was, it wasn't safe no matter where Paige was. As long as the Moonlight Strangler was after her, Matthew was in danger, too, because the killer could use Matthew to get to her. Besides, he didn't have a right to keep Paige from their son.

However, he did have a right to make rules for this visit.

"I'll start making arrangements for a safe house for you," Jax informed her. "Come on," he said. "Let's go see Matthew before I change my mind."

Chapter Six

Chaos. That was the one word Paige could think of when Jax took the final turn toward the Crockett ranch. A place that'd once been her home.

Well, it sure didn't look like home now.

The cops and CSIs were there. The medical examiner's van, too. Blue lights whirled, and the yellow crime scene tape snapped and rattled in the hot summer breeze.

Before the attack a year earlier, she'd been a CSI for almost a decade, since finishing college, and she'd been part of situations just like this. Had been in the middle of one as well when she'd been left for dead. But it was different now since she'd been the cause of this particular scene. One man was dead and another in the hospital, and Jax and she had barely escaped with their lives.

And it wasn't the end.

No. The text proved that.

This isn't over.

Paige hadn't needed the text to tell her that, though.

She suspected this nightmare was just getting started, and she needed to figure out what her next step was.

Jax was no doubt doing the same thing.

Along with dealing with her return from the dead.

Other than a few internet searches, she hadn't kept tabs on his life. That wasn't only a safety precaution but also to preserve what was left of her heart and sanity. Just that earlier glance of Matthew with Belinda had sent Paige's emotions into a tailspin. She'd lost so much the day she'd nearly lost her life.

Matthew.

And Jax.

Though Jax hadn't been hers to lose. After countless arguments over her refusal to stop investigating the Moonlight Strangler, they'd separated. Paige just hadn't been able to let go of the case, and that thirst for justice had cost her Jax.

They had signed divorce papers the day of the attack. Ironic. Or maybe that'd been the Moonlight Strangler's plan all along, to wait until she was at the lowest point of her life to strike. To squeeze out every last drop of misery before he choked her to death.

Jax didn't stay on the road, though his house was less than a quarter of a mile away. He maneuvered the cruiser through a cattle gate in the pasture and drove onto a ranch trail. No doubt to avoid disturbing the scene that the CSIs were investigating. The truck explosion had likely scattered debris everywhere, and each little fragment could give them clues as to who'd built the bomb and set it.

"You've added more livestock," she remarked.

Small talk. It almost seemed insulting, considering they had some very serious things to discuss, but with her frayed nerves and the pain pounding in her head, it was the best Paige could manage.

He made a grunt of agreement. Clearly no small talk for him, but his jaw muscles were at war against each other. Probably his thoughts, too. Jax didn't want her here, and he might let her stay only a few minutes. That was okay as long as she got to spend those few minutes with Matthew.

After he'd cleared the crime scene, Jax pulled back onto the private road that led to the ranch, and his house came into view. Of course, she knew exactly what it looked like. The two-story stone and wood house. None of the lights were on, a security precaution no doubt. This way, a sniper wouldn't be able to see anyone inside. She'd already heard Jax arrange to have the area searched to make sure there weren't any other hired guns lurking around.

It wasn't as large as the main house that was just up the road, but it was still big. Six bedrooms. When Jax and she had first married, they'd joked they would fill every one of those rooms with kids.

Once, she'd been welcome here, but there were no welcoming vibes from Jax now. Just the opposite. He didn't want her here. And Paige wasn't sure she wanted to be here, either. Anything she did right now could put her precious little boy in danger.

Or anything she didn't do.

There was just no way of knowing how the Moon-light Strangler would try to come after her next.

"How much time do I have?" she asked when he pulled the cruiser to a stop.

"Not much."

Since he didn't hesitate, he'd obviously been thinking about how all of this would play out, and Paige would have to go along with whatever demands he made. Before she'd faked her death, Jax and she had worked out a split custody agreement, but with the danger and her yearlong absence, she didn't have any claim to custody.

For now, anyway.

Jax parked the cruiser directly in front of the house in the circular drive. She immediately spotted two ranch hands in the yard. Both armed. One was Teddy McQueen, someone she'd known most of her life, and he gave Paige a semiwelcoming nod. She didn't recognize the other hand, a reminder that some things had indeed changed in the past year.

That thought caused her to freeze for a moment.

Was Jax seeing anyone? Or more, was he in a serious relationship?

She hated the pang of jealousy that coiled inside her. She'd made her bed, and now she had to lie in it. And she wouldn't be lying in it with Jax.

They got out of the cruiser, started up the steps, but the door opened before they even reached it. Yet another familiar face. Levi. And unlike the others she'd encountered tonight, he flashed her a quick smile and hugged her once she was safe inside.

"You both okay?" Levi asked, his attention going to the stitches on her head before he glanced at his brother and then reset the security system.

"We're alive," Jax answered.

Levi nodded and hitched his thumb toward the hall. "Chase is in Matthew's room."

Good. Like all of Jax's brothers, Chase was a law-man. A marshal. And he would put his life on the line to protect Matthew. All of them would.

Later, if there was a later, Paige wanted to catch up with Levi. Alexa, too. For now, she settled for whisper-ing congrats on his engagement to the woman who'd once been Paige's best friend. Paige wasn't sure how Alexa would feel about her now, though, especially since Jax said Alexa had been beating herself up about a death that hadn't even happened.

"One of the hands drove behind Belinda when she went home," Levi explained as they headed toward the hall. "No one followed them."

Jax made another of those grunts, this one of ap-proval. Paige hadn't been sure what Belinda's living arrangements were, but she obviously didn't live with Jax if she'd been escorted home.

The moment they reached the hall, she saw Chase. He was sitting in the doorway of the nursery. No smile or hug from him. His hard eyes condemned her and dismissed her with a single glance before he turned his attention to Jax.

"Matthew's asleep," Chase whispered.

Paige automatically checked the time on her phone. It was nearly 9:00 p.m., but she wasn't even sure if this was his regular bedtime or not. She prayed he hadn't been afraid when he'd heard those shots and the sirens.

Almost hesitantly, Chase stepped out of the way so she could enter. Just like that, Paige's heart thudded against her chest and her breath became thin with each step that brought her closer to her son. He wasn't sleeping in a crib but rather a bed with railings, another reminder that she'd lost so much time with him.

Paige knelt on the floor so she could get a better look at his face. She didn't dare ask Jax to turn on the light. For one thing, it might not be a safe thing to do, and for another he might not want to be accommodating.

She reached out, touched her fingers to his hair. He still had those baby curls. Still had his daddy's face. But she could see some of herself in him, too. The blond hair and the shape of his mouth.

Paige couldn't stop the tears that sprang to her eyes. Couldn't stop herself from brushing a kiss on Matthew's cheek, either. She kept it soft, but it must not have been soft enough because Matthew stirred, and his eyes popped open.

Jax grumbled something under his breath. Something she didn't catch. But he clearly wasn't happy about this. Matthew, however, didn't seem upset at all. His gaze went from Paige to his dad and uncles before his attention settled on her.

"Mommy," Matthew said.

Paige couldn't have been more shocked, and she looked back at Jax for an explanation.

Jax shrugged. "I've shown him your picture." He glanced at the nightstand, but the only thing there was a lamp and baby monitor. "It's usually right there by his bed." He went closer, searching through the drawer. No picture. "Belinda must have moved it."

Maybe Belinda had taken it with her when she'd moved Matthew into the bathroom during the attack. At least Paige liked to think that Belinda wanted Matthew to know who his mother was.

"Thank you for showing it to him," Paige managed to say, though she wasn't sure how her little boy recognized her from an old picture. Not with this brunette hair.

But Paige didn't waste any time trying to figure that out. She studied her son's face, soaking in every feature and committing it to memory.

"Mommy's here," she whispered to him.

Matthew smiled in that lazy, no-effort kind of way that reminded her of Jax, but his eyelids immediately started to drift back down. She sat there, trying to hang on to each precious moment, but they slipped away so quickly, and it took only a matter of seconds before Matthew was asleep again.

"We need to talk," Jax said, motioning for her to follow him.

She did, but Paige didn't take her eyes off Matthew as she made her way to the door. She continued to look at him until he was no longer in sight. Maybe, just maybe, this wouldn't be the last time she'd ever see him.

Chase took up his guard position by Matthew's door again, and Levi disappeared into another part of the house. No doubt to give Jax and her some time alone so he could deliver whatever bad news he was about to tell her. And it would be bad. Paige could tell by his expression. That was the problem with knowing him so well.

Jax led her to the other side of the house and into the family room. Someone had redecorated it with a fresh coat of soft gold paint and new furniture that looked more kid-proof than the leather set they'd once had in there. The most noticeable change, though, was that their wedding pictures were missing from the mantel.

"I'll take you to the safe house as soon as Jericho has it set up," he said.

No surprise about that. She'd heard Jax talking to Jericho about it on the drive over. Considering how Jericho felt about her, he was probably working at lightning speed to get the house ready so that Jax wouldn't have to be under the same roof as her.

He motioned for her to sit on the sofa. An invitation, of sorts, and yet another reminder that this wasn't her home. Not that she needed such a reminder. It was obvious Jax had erased her. Well, except for that photo he'd been showing Matthew.

"You'll need to stay at the safe house until Jericho and I can find the Moonlight Strangler," Jax added.

Which meant she could be locked away for years.

Not exactly what she wanted. "But what about Matthew? And you? You need a safe house, too."

He nodded. "I'm working on that, as well. My plan is to move Matthew first thing in the morning, and we'll lock down the ranch. Chase, Jericho and Addie all have children now, and I have to make sure none of this danger spills over onto them."

Paige couldn't agree more. However, she didn't want her son living with this dark cloud always following him.

"If we don't get answers from Loveland," she said, "then I need to set some kind of trap for the Moonlight Strangler."

Jax was already shaking his head and mumbling some profanity before she even finished. "That didn't work so well tonight. No, you'll stay put in the safe house while I work this investigation." His eyes narrowed. "And this time, you'll listen."

Paige deserved that last dig. Jax had warned her too many times about involving herself in the Moonlight Strangler investigation, and she hadn't listened. Look where that'd gotten her.

"I'm sure Cord is working on some kind of plan," she continued. "You might want to call him to make sure you two don't get in each other's way."

Of course, Cord would consider anything that Jax did as getting in his way. Still, she didn't want Jax or Cord caught in each other's cross fire if they did manage to trap the killer.

Jax didn't agree to her request to call Cord, but he

did ease down in the chair across from her so they would have direct eye contact. "Start from the beginning and tell me everything about who helped you fake your death, who helped you afterward and finish by explaining how the Moonlight Strangler found out you were alive."

Paige took a long, deep breath because she figured she'd need it. "Like I already told you, Leland helped. He was on duty that night, arrived at the scene and got in the ambulance with me. He talked the doctor at the San Antonio hospital into going along with it. The doctor's name is Wesley Nolan. He had me transferred under an alias to a hospital in Houston, and I recovered there."

Well, her body had recovered, anyway.

"So, who did we bury in the family cemetery?" Jax asked.

"A cadaver of a homeless woman. Dr. Nolan told the funeral home to have a closed casket service because my injuries were too severe for a viewing."

"This Dr. Nolan went above and beyond. I'd like to know why. I want to talk to him."

She sighed. "Don't bother looking for him. He died in a car accident a couple of months ago."

That got his attention. "Accident?"

She knew why he was asking. One of the three people who'd helped her was now dead. "Cord checked into it, and he said it didn't look suspicious." Of course, that didn't mean the Moonlight Strangler or even someone else hadn't made it look like an accident.

"How'd Cord get involved?" Jax snapped, sounding like a lawman. Strange, because he usually didn't. He was the lawman Jericho used in interrogations when they wanted to coax out a confession without the criminal even realizing he was being interrogated. Of course, Jax wasn't personally involved with those interrogations.

"I contacted him after I got settled in Houston. I knew he was investigating his birth father, and I thought he could help me find him before you or Matthew were in any danger."

The flat look he gave her let her know that it'd been a huge mistake on her part. And it had been. She'd tried to exclude Jax from her life so she could protect Matthew and him, but that had obviously backfired.

"So how do you think the Moonlight Strangler found out you were alive?" Jax went on. "You said it was possible that Leland let something slip."

She nodded. "Because at the time, Leland was the only person who knew where I was. I did ask him about it, and he said he'd been careful when he visited me and had made sure no one followed him."

"He *visited* you?" Jax asked.

Paige opened her mouth, closed it and decided to take a moment to figure out what Jax's tone meant. Was he jealous? No. It couldn't be that. This was about her trusting Leland instead of him.

"Leland was the one who helped me move from the hospital to the safe house in the Panhandle where I stayed while I was recovering. Then, when I was well enough to work, he got me a job doing computer background checks for a security agency that vets corporate executives," she explained. "His friend owns the agency, and Leland told him that he was the one doing the work."

"Leland really went out of his way for you," Jax said. His tone was flat, but that wasn't a flat look in his eyes.

"I needed money, and I couldn't very well access my old savings accounts. Anyway, Leland helped me get a fake ID and he found a small apartment for me in Houston. He'd drive over every other week from San Antonio and pay me in cash for the work I did."

There was some part of that explanation Jax obviously didn't like because his mouth tightened, and she got another glare from him. "At any point did it occur to you to call me, or maybe even Chase? He's a marshal and could have gotten you into official protective custody."

"Of course it occurred to me. I've already told you that it did, but I was afraid I'd get Matthew and you killed."

She had to fight the tears again, and she cursed them. Mercy, she already felt so bruised and weak, and she didn't want to be crying in front of Jax. Evidently, he didn't want her crying, either, because he cursed again and leaned closer. For a moment she thought he might lend her a shoulder, but his phone buzzed, and the moment was lost. Which was just as well. The last place she needed to be was in Jax's arms.

Even if her body thought it was a good idea.

"It's Jericho," he said, glancing at the screen, and he put the call on speaker. Probably because he wanted her to hear details of the safe house—a place he likely couldn't wait to take her. Anything to get her out of his house.

"Bad news," Jericho greeted. "And that's bad news on more than one front. Loveland's dead. He never regained consciousness, never uttered a word about who hired him to attack you and Paige."

That didn't help her fight the tears, but Paige blinked them back. It'd been a long shot, anyway. Even if Loveland had lived, he might not have ratted out his boss.

Of course, now she had to live with the fact that she'd killed a man. She'd done that to stop him from hurting Jax and her, but still, it settled like a dead weight in her chest.

"What else is wrong?" Jax asked his brother when Jericho didn't continue.

Jericho's hesitation had her moving to the edge of the seat. Not that she was especially eager to hear another round of bad news, but she didn't want to miss a word of what he had to say.

"The safe house is ready," Jericho finally said, "but you won't be able to take Paige there. Not tonight, anyway. I don't think it's a good idea for you to leave the house with her right now. Not until I've had someone check the area."

Paige met Jax's gaze to see if he knew what this was all about, but he only shook his head. "What's going on, Jericho?" Jax pressed.

"I got a weird text about five minutes ago. I'm sending you a screenshot."

Paige hurried to Jax's side so she could see the message for herself. "'Tell Jax that I'm watching Paige and him. Love how he parked the cop car right in front of his house so that she didn't have to be out in the open. Bet she appreciated Levi opening the door for her, too,'" she read aloud.

Oh, God. Whoever had sent the message, either the Moonlight Strangler or Pittman, was close. Close enough to see their every move.

"'Yeah, I saw it all,'" Jax continued to read. "'And I'll keep on seeing every move Paige makes. Tell her that soon she'll be dead for good.'"

Chapter Seven

The sound woke Jax. Not that he was fully asleep, anyway. But despite the fact that the sound was barely a whisper, it made it through the cobwebs in his head, and he sprang to his feet and grabbed his holster from the nightstand.

Damn it. What was wrong now?

Since it was barely 5:00 a.m., he figured neither Paige nor Matthew should be up yet. Chase should be asleep, too, since he was barely an hour off watch detail. Levi would be up, taking his turn at making sure they were all safe, but he shouldn't be whispering to anyone at this hour unless something had come up.

Jax was already dressed. For the most part, anyway. After he'd pulled a shift to keep watch, he'd changed clothes but not to his usual sleeping boxers. He'd put on fresh jeans and a shirt in case they had to make a quick escape, but his shirt was unbuttoned, and he was barefoot.

"It's Paige," Levi said the moment Jax stepped into

the hall. His brother tipped his head in the direction of Matthew's room.

Jax's heartbeat went into overdrive. Not only because Paige was apparently in Matthew's room but because the sound Jax had heard was of someone crying. Matthew maybe.

He ran, skidding to a stop on the hardwood floors, and what Jax saw wasn't anything compared to the worst-case scenario he'd built up in his head. Paige was sitting on the floor. Not near Matthew but on the other side of the nursery. Matthew was still sacked out, and Paige was watching him.

Well, watching him through her tears and soft sobs.

Her head whipped up, her gaze colliding with Jax's, and she waved him off. Maybe her attempt to get him to leave. As if that was going to happen. He holstered his gun, went to her and helped her to her feet.

"I've ruined everything," she said.

Jax didn't argue with her, though he had to admit this wasn't her fault. Most of it, anyway. But she didn't need to hear him say that right now since she was obviously beating herself up.

Judging from the hoarseness of her voice and her red eyes, she'd been crying for a long time. And she likely hadn't slept.

He'd lent her some pj's—a Christmas present that he'd never used—but they looked as wrinkle-free as they had when he'd taken them out of the package and given them to her. There were also dark circles under her eyes. Circles that were nearly the same color as the nasty bruise that was now on her forehead.

So, with all of that, how the hell did she still manage to look so good?

Probably because he was still attracted to her. He always had been, and certain mindless parts of his body just weren't going to let him forget it.

Jax went over and helped her to her feet. "Come on. I'll make you a cup of tea if I can find some." After the divorce, he'd cleared out her stash of the Irish breakfast tea she bought in bulk, but he might have missed some.

Since Paige wasn't too steady on her feet, Jax hooked his arm around her waist and got her moving. Past Levi, who gave him a raised eyebrow. Maybe at the close contact.

Jax gave him a raised eyebrow right back for that hug he'd given Paige the night before. Jax wasn't jealous that his brother had done that, but this situation was already complicated enough without giving Paige the full-court welcome back home.

"It really hit me this morning," she said, wiping away the endless stream of tears. "I've lost so much time with him. Too much."

Yes, she had. Again, Jax didn't voice that. He got her headed in the direction of the kitchen, cursing the fact that the house suddenly seemed gigantic with miles and miles of floor space. That probably had plenty to do with the fact that he didn't want to keep her in his arms any longer than necessary.

"All that time I spent investigating the Moonlight

Strangler," she went on. "I kept at it, knowing it was causing a rift between us."

It was an understatement, and at the root of it was that she just couldn't let go of something that Jax had known could be dangerous. It was something she should have trusted him to investigate, but she hadn't.

Lack of trust was his hot button.

Giving up had been an equally hot button for her.

Not a good combination when both were putting in so many hours with the baby and at work that they didn't have time for each other. Jax would accept his blame for part of that, but this whole faked death thing was on Paige's shoulders.

When they finally made it to the kitchen, Jax put her at the breakfast table and went in search of that tea. Nada. He had vague memories of getting drunker than a skunk and tossing everything that would remind her of him.

Everything except that picture he'd put in Matthew's room.

He gave up his search, got a pot of coffee brewing and made a check out the window. Something he'd been doing most of the night. A team of ranch hands was out there, patrolling, and there'd be a team in place until he moved Paige and Matthew. Hopefully, that would happen soon.

When the coffee was finished, he set both a cup and a box of tissues on the table in front of her, but Paige just stared at them. Stared, and then she got to her feet.

"Just please hold me a second," she said.

That was the only warning Jax got before she was in his arms.

Instant jolt of memories. Really strong ones. His body immediately started to prepare itself for Paige. And not a good preparation, either. His body was smacking the foreplay label on this and reminding him that it'd been way too long since he'd had her in his arms.

And in his bed.

Jax didn't push her away, though. Mainly because this wasn't anywhere near foreplay for her. She was falling apart right in front of him, and he felt his arms close around her before he could talk himself out of it.

"I'm sorry," she said.

The latest apology put his teeth on edge. No way could an apology erase what she'd done. For nearly a year he'd grieved for her. Cursed her. Because he'd believed she had caused her own death. Now he was cursing her for lying to him. Cursing her because of this blasted attraction that just wouldn't die.

She eased back, her gaze finding his, and she looked down between them. At his bare chest.

Where she had her hand.

Paige didn't exactly jump back, but she did step away from him and mumbled yet another apology that he didn't want to hear. She also wiped away the tears, and this time they stayed gone. Jax could almost see her steeling herself. Maybe to fight off the attraction. Maybe because she just didn't want him to see her cry.

"I promise I won't go crazy on you," she said. "I just

need to get my footing and figure out how to catch the Moonlight Strangler."

Definitely more like the old Paige now. Except this time, he totally understood her obsession to catch this particular killer. Because this time his son was the one in the crosshairs.

"There's nothing new on the investigation," he told her, and Jax got himself a cup of coffee. "But I've been giving some thought to that last text. Why send it to Jericho? We know the Moonlight Strangler has your phone number because he's been texting you, and you said he included details of the attack that only a few people knew."

She stayed quiet a moment and nodded. "You think that text to Jericho was from Darrin Pittman?"

Now it was his turn to nod. "Whoever sent it used a burner cell, one that can't be traced, of course. But even if Darrin wasn't the one behind the attack last night, he's probably heard you're alive."

"One of the Unknown Caller texts could have been from him." She took out her phone from the pocket of the pj's and showed him the cache of calls and texts.

Unknown caller, Cord and Leland.

Jax couldn't help but notice that she had four missed calls from Leland, and they'd all come since she had been back at the ranch.

"I let Leland's calls go to voice mail," she said, putting her phone away. "I wasn't up to talking to him."

There. He heard it again. Something in her tone.

It'd been there the night before when the cop's name had come up.

"Is there anything about Leland that you're not telling me?" he came out and asked.

Paige gave a heavy sigh and sank back down into the chair. "We, uh, had a parting of the ways."

"What the heck does that mean?" Jax pressed when she didn't continue.

Another sigh, and she didn't make eye contact. "I told you that Leland had been helping me. Well, he started to develop feelings for me— again. Feelings I could never return, and I told him that."

Jax took a moment to process that. "I'm guessing Leland was upset?"

She made a sound to indicate that that was an understatement. "He didn't say anything to me. He just walked out the same way he did after I broke things off with him years ago." Now her gaze came to his. "All of that happened right before the Moonlight Strangler contacted me to set up the meeting. And no, I don't believe Leland told him."

Maybe. "Then it's a helluva coincidence, especially since Leland was only one of two people who had your phone number at that time."

"That still doesn't mean he gave the number to a killer. Or to Pittman. Yes, Leland was upset and hurt, but I don't think he would have set me up to die."

The jury was still out on that as far as Jax was concerned, and he took out his phone to text Jericho and let him know he should call Leland in for an interview.

However, the sound of a car engine stopped him, and Jax hurried to the window. It was a vehicle he recognized.

Belinda's.

And it was indeed the nanny all right. Hard to miss that gold-blond hair when she stepped from the car.

She normally arrived at his place around this time of morning so he could do some ranch work before going into the sheriff's office. However, with everything that'd gone on the night before, Jax had made it clear that she should stay away until he had some things settled.

Jax buttoned his shirt and went to the back door to temporarily disarm the security system. By the time he did that, Belinda was already on the porch.

"I couldn't wait," she said, her breath rushing out. "I had to make sure Matthew and you were all right."

"We're fine." Jax stepped back for her to enter only so he could shut the door and turn the security system back on. That way, if a hired gun did manage to sneak past the hands, at least Jax would know if there was a break-in, since all the doors and windows were wired.

Belinda immediately pulled him into her arms. His second hug of the morning, and Jax didn't want this one any more than he'd wanted the other one. Of course, the one from Paige still had the heat simmering in his body. This one from Belinda had him stepping back.

She noticed.

So did Paige, judging from the way her gaze shifted between Belinda and him. She probably wanted to know if Belinda was more than just Matthew's nanny. She wasn't. But Belinda had made it pretty clear that she wanted to be a whole lot more.

Belinda's attention landed on Paige, specifically the pj's, and because Jax was watching her so closely, he saw the flicker of disapproval go through Belinda's pale blue eyes. Once, Belinda and Paige had been friends. They'd all gone to high school together, but the tension in the air wasn't so friendly right now. Paige stood slowly, adjusting her pj's and looking as uncomfortable about this situation as Jax felt.

"Paige," Belinda said. Not exactly a warm greeting. "How could you have done this to Jax? And how could you come back into his life now after all this time? He'd gotten over you. He was moving on with his life. And now you've brought danger right to his doorstep."

"She didn't have a say in that attack," Jax told Belinda when Paige stayed quiet. But he wanted to groan. Now he was defending Paige. Great. Just great.

Belinda's bottom lip started to tremble and her eyes watered. "I prayed it wasn't you I saw yesterday by the garage."

Jax pulled back his shoulders. "You saw Paige?"

It was a really easy question, but it still took Belinda several long moments to answer. "Yes. I was on the porch swing with Matthew and I got a glimpse of someone. Maybe her, but I also thought maybe it was a friend of Buddy's or one of the other hands."

Paige looked surprised, but Jax figured he had her

beat in the surprise department. "And you didn't tell me that you thought you might have seen her?" he snapped.

Belinda blinked. "I was hoping it wasn't her. Not that I wanted her dead," she quickly added. "But I didn't want her to come back. I figured if she was alive, then the Moonlight Strangler would still be after her. I was right, wasn't I?"

Maybe.

Jax didn't doubt for a minute that the Moonlight Strangler would want to finish what he'd started, but Jax wasn't convinced the killer was the only player here.

"Did you break into the house, too?" Belinda asked, looking at Paige.

"W-what?" Paige shook her head and turned to Jax. "You had a break-in?"

Jax's hands went on his hips. "This is the first I'm hearing about it. When did this happen?"

The tension in the room went up a significant notch. "Yesterday afternoon. While you were at work, I took Matthew out to see the new horses. I was only gone for about thirty minutes, but when I came back in, I saw that someone had…damaged Paige's picture, the one you usually keep next to Matthew's bed."

"Damaged?" Paige and he asked in unison.

Belinda didn't jump to answer, but she went to the junk drawer and took out the framed photo. It was indeed the one of Paige, and there was "damage" all right.

The glass had been shattered, and it appeared that either the glass—or someone—had cut Paige's face.

Not an ordinary cut, either. There was a gash on the cheek, very similar to the real one the Moonlight Strangler had given her.

Jax cursed, and Paige staggered back a step.

"Why wouldn't you have told me about this?" Jax demanded of Belinda.

More tears sprang to Belinda's eyes. "At first, I thought it had fallen off the table. Or that maybe you'd gotten upset and did it."

"I wasn't here," Jax reminded her. "You knew I was at work."

He tried not to sound furious with her, but he was. This was huge. It could have meant someone had indeed broken in. Or rather just walked in, because he doubted Belinda had locked up to take Matthew to see the horses.

Her tears turned to sobs. "Don't be upset with me. I thought maybe you'd come back home for something, that you saw the picture and decided it was finally time to put Paige out of yours and Matthew's lives."

"I'll always be part of his life," Paige whispered. Not angry but rather hurt. "Even if I'm not here, I'll always be his mother."

Belinda's face turned red, and her nostrils flared. She looked ready to scream or do something Jax was sure they'd all regret. Emotions were running sky high right now, and he needed to diffuse it.

"Was anything else broken or taken?" Jax asked her, not only because he wanted to know but also because he would get them talking about this potential break-in rather than Paige.

Belinda's glare stayed on Paige for a while before she finally shook her head. "Nothing that I found. Nothing else seemed to be out of place."

So, why would someone break in only to destroy a photo of Paige? Jax figured he knew the answer to that, and it was an answer he didn't like one bit.

"You should go home now," he told Belinda.

She frantically shook her head. "But Matthew—"

"Will be fine," he interrupted. Jax hoped that was true, anyway. "I'll call you later when I have some things settled."

Belinda took hold of his arm and opened her mouth as if she might argue about staying. But then she glanced at Paige, the anger returning to Belinda's eyes. "You'd be a fool to get involved with her again. Just remember how she broke your heart and don't let it happen again."

And with that crystal-clear warning, Belinda walked out. Or rather she stormed out.

Jax went back to the window to watch her leave. "She's not usually this, well, emotional." Not the exact word he wanted to use, but at least it didn't include any profanity.

"She's in love with you," Paige provided.

This would have been a really good time for him to deny it. But he couldn't. Because it was almost certainly true.

He was about to assure Paige that he hadn't encouraged Belinda's feelings, but he stopped himself. Saying something like that might only encourage this blasted attraction between Paige and him.

That attraction already had enough steam without his adding more.

"I didn't break in," Paige insisted. "And I certainly wouldn't have done this to my own photo." She paused. "But maybe Belinda did."

Again, it would have been a good time to deny that, but it was indeed possible. Jax hated that he could even consider that Belinda would do something like that. He trusted her with his son's life. His safety. And if Belinda was coming unglued over the prospect of Paige's return, then he didn't want her anywhere near Matthew. Telling her that, though, would go over like a lead balloon.

"Maybe the picture just fell the way Belinda suggested," Paige added. "Maybe." But she didn't sound any more certain about that than Jax.

Since the picture seemed to turn Paige's stomach—it was doing that to him, too—he put it facedown on the counter. "I'll have it checked for prints and traces just in case." Though any evidence had likely already been destroyed.

Paige shuddered and scrubbed her hands down her arms. "If the Moonlight Strangler was really here in the house…" She didn't finish that. No need. Jax was right there with her at that sickening thought.

Was this part of the warped game he'd been playing with Paige?

Jax's phone buzzed, and he was so on edge that the

sound startled him. But it was only Jericho. Maybe calling with good news, because heaven help them, they needed it.

"I got another text," Jericho said the moment Jax answered.

Damn. He knew from his brother's tone that this was from the killer. Or else someone pretending to be the killer. Either way, it definitely wouldn't fall into the good-news category.

"Want me to send a screenshot or just read it?" Jericho asked.

"Read it." Jax doubted Paige wanted to see anything else that was stomach-turning. That's also why he didn't put the call on speaker. He could give Paige a sanitized version of the message afterward.

"'Tell Paige that I hope she's enjoying her visit with your son's nanny,'" Jericho read. "'Guess it didn't go well, considering how Belinda sped away.'"

"He's watching us," Jax said on the tail end of a single word of profanity.

"Yeah. And the CSIs used infrared to search the area around your house." Jericho paused. "That means there are probably cameras somewhere. Small ones that the CSIs missed. There shouldn't be any snipers because we set up sensors to alert us if anyone is hiding out in those trees near your house. If the sensors are triggered, the alarm at the main house will sound, and one of the hands will call you right away."

Good. Though it was a precaution that Jax hoped

they didn't need. Especially since he'd be moving Paige soon.

Hell, he hoped so, anyway.

"I'm sending the CSIs out there now to check for cameras," Jericho continued. "I'll have them go through the cruiser and the other vehicles as well, but you can have the hands go ahead and start looking, too."

It was something Jax should have already thought to check, especially since it wouldn't have been that hard for someone to attach a camera or tracking device. However, it was possible someone had done that when they broke in.

"I'll need the house checked, too," Jax added. "And I'm bringing in a photo that I need processed for evidence." He was about to explain what had happened, or rather what had possibly happened, but a sound stopped him.

Two cars were approaching.

After the run-in he'd just had with Belinda, at first he thought the woman was returning for another conversation. But these weren't vehicles he recognized. This was a sleek silver sports car and a blue pickup truck.

"I'll call you back," he told Jericho and then glanced at Paige. "Stay away from the window." And Jax drew his gun.

But she didn't stay back. She hurried to the fridge, took the gun that he had stashed there and looked out just as the man stepped from the car.

"Oh, God," Paige said under her breath. "What's he doing here?"

Jax intended to find out. And fast. Because their tall, blond-haired visitor was none other than Darrin Pittman.

Hell. What now?

Jax also recognized the other much smaller man who threw open the truck door. So did Paige.

"Leland," she grumbled, clearly not happy.

Neither was Jax. This was yet someone else he didn't want near Matthew, Paige or his home.

Leland got out of his truck, and in the same motion, he drew his gun. And he aimed it right at Darrin.

Chapter Eight

Paige wasn't in the mood to deal with either Darrin or Leland, much less both of them at once. And she certainly didn't want to face them while still wearing Jax's pajamas.

"Will Leland shoot Darrin?" Jax asked her.

"Possibly." It was sad that she didn't know for sure. "Leland knows that Darrin harassed and threatened me. And Leland's got somewhat of a short fuse. Stall them. I'll talk to them after I've changed."

Jax looked at her as if she'd sprouted some extra noses. "You're not going out there."

She appreciated his attempt to protect her, but she was going to have to overrule him on this. "I want to find out if Darrin was behind the attack last night, and he's far more likely to say something to me than to you or Leland. Even if what he says is out of anger."

Except it wasn't anger when it came to Darrin. More like blind rage.

"Make sure someone's with Matthew," she said to Jax, maybe insulting him, since it was so obvious.

Still, she didn't want to take any chances with Matthew's safety, especially since there were so many other things about this dangerous situation that they couldn't control.

Paige didn't wait for Jax to respond to or argue with her. She hurried back to the guest room and practically threw on jeans and a top. No change of clothes. She'd cleared all of her personal things out during the divorce, but Jax had washed and dried her things after lending her his pj's.

She kept the gun she'd taken from the fridge and prayed she didn't have to use it. While she was praying, she added that maybe Matthew would sleep through all of this.

"I'm ready," she said, racing back to the kitchen.

But Jax wasn't there. Levi was, though. He was in the back doorway. She huffed when she glanced out the window and spotted Jax in the side yard. He, too, had his gun drawn.

"Jax says I'm supposed to keep you inside," Levi warned her.

The flat look she gave him must have made him realize this was a battle he'd lose, because he cursed and stepped aside. She got another scowl and some unspoken profanity from Jax when she walked out onto the back porch.

"You shouldn't be out here," Leland shouted to her. Other than a glance, he didn't actually look at her. He kept his attention, and gun, nailed to Darrin.

"He's right," Jax agreed, his gaze sweeping all

around them. Levi and the ranch hands were doing the same.

Paige didn't go out in the yard. She stayed on the porch and wished that Jax would do the same. No such luck. He was right out there where he could be gunned down.

If Darrin cared one ounce about being held at gunpoint, or being out in the open with a killer loose, he didn't show it, and unlike Leland he kept his gaze on her.

And Darrin smiled.

That sick smile she'd seen him dole out too many times before he issued a veiled threat or called her some vile name. She'd told Jax the truth about Leland having a temper, but it was as cold as ice compared to Darrin's.

It'd been a year since she'd seen Darrin. He certainly hadn't been smiling at her then. He'd been threatening her with yet another lawsuit and with bodily harm. But other than that, he hadn't changed. He was still driving a pricey car. Still wearing those high-end preppy clothes. Probably still living off his trust fund and assaulting women any chance he got. There was a string of women who'd made complaints against him for sexual assault, but the complaints always disappeared when his daddy paid off people in the legal system.

All but one.

The rape charge where Paige had collected the evidence. That was the start of this whole nightmare with Darrin.

"Why are you here?" Paige asked, aiming the question at Darrin, but she also glanced at Leland to let him know she wanted an answer from him, as well.

"Visiting you, of course," Darrin said, that smile still on his face. The morning breeze tossed his fashionably rumpled hair. "Back from the dead, I see, but you're looking a little beat-up there, Paige. What? Did you piss off the wrong person and get smacked around? That bruise and scar look good on you."

"Shut up," Leland warned him. He continued to stand there, his gun aimed at Darrin.

"Both of you shut up," Jax warned Leland and Darrin right back. "Neither of you should be here. This is private property, and you're trespassing."

Leland flinched as if Jax had slugged him. Maybe because he expected cooperation from a brother in blue? But after the attack, Jax wasn't in a trusting mood, and it probably didn't help that Leland was her old flame.

"Just taking a detour," Darrin said. "Your brother, the sheriff, told me to come in for questioning." Now his gaze narrowed when he looked at Paige. "Guess you've been telling lies about me again?"

"No need. The truth will get you in more trouble than any lie I can make up. You raped a woman."

"Not according to the law." Darrin outstretched his arms. "I'm free as a bird."

"Not for long if I have anything to say about it," Leland volunteered. "I was on my way into town to talk to the sheriff, and I spotted this clown heading out here.

I figured he was looking for Paige so he could cause some trouble."

"I was looking for her," Darrin readily admitted. "But not to cause trouble. I just wanted to welcome her home. And to let her know that I'm ready to do whatever it takes to clear my name. That involves getting her to tell the truth about that so-called evidence."

Paige couldn't help it. She laughed. Not from humor, but from the absurdity of his threat. "Someone wants me dead. Clearing your name isn't anywhere on my list of things to do. Unless, of course, you're the one who orchestrated the attack against us last night."

Darrin shrugged, but she thought maybe she'd hit a nerve. Of course, Paige had no idea if that was because he was truly innocent of the attack or if he was riled that she'd figured him out so easily.

"Let's end this so that Paige can go inside," Jax said. He tipped his head to Darrin. "You get back in your car now and leave. Go straight to the sheriff's office so you can be charged with trespassing and any other charge I can come up with."

Paige thought Darrin would argue with that, but he glanced around at the five guns aimed at him and must have considered that staying just wasn't a bright idea.

Darrin threw open his car door, his glare going right to Paige. "This isn't over."

The words went through her like knives. Because it was the exact threat the Moonlight Strangler had made to her.

Or had he?

She'd been so certain that the texts had been from the true serial killer, but maybe it'd all been a hoax set up by none other than Darrin. Of course, it didn't make this situation any less deadly.

Darrin started his car and sped off, gunning the engine so that the tires kicked up some pebbles right at Leland. Leland sidestepped them, but what he didn't do was get in his truck and follow Darrin. Instead, he came closer to the porch.

"I need to talk to Paige," Leland said. His tone wasn't that of a tough cop. Nor was it directed at her. He looked at Jax when he spoke, and he was clearly bargaining with a fellow officer.

"Why don't we all go inside," Leland continued, "so Paige isn't out in the open? There could be snipers in the area."

"The area's been cleared," Jax snapped.

Maybe it would stay that way. Of course, the threat could be standing in front of them. Except Paige wasn't sure she believed it. Darrin clearly wanted to do her harm. Ditto for the Moonlight Strangler. And Belinda probably just wanted her to disappear again. But Leland had actually helped her.

"I'll talk to him," Paige told Jax.

Oh, Jax did not like that, but she tried to silently convey to him that she wanted to question Leland to see if he knew anything about the attack.

The seconds crawled by, and she watched Jax have a debate with himself. She also saw the moment he conceded.

"Holster your gun," Jax ordered Leland. "You've got five minutes, so talk fast. And you're not going inside. Anything you say can be said on the porch."

However, Jax did come onto the porch, and he maneuvered her into the doorway so she'd be more protected. And so that he'd be partially in front of her.

Jax leaned in closer to Levi. "Ask the ranch hands to start searching the cruiser and the other vehicles for cameras or tracking devices," Jax instructed. "I need to make sure they're clean in case we have to leave fast. I also want them to check the exterior of the house."

With that task out of the way, Jax turned back to Leland, but Leland was staring at her now. Maybe glaring, too.

"I'm not here to hurt you," Leland told her. "I want to help you, something I've been doing for months now."

"Yeah, she told me all about that," Jax snapped. "She also told me you two recently had a parting of the ways."

Leland flinched. Clearly hurt that she'd confided in Jax about something that he would see as a personal matter between them. And maybe she'd been wrong to tell Jax. Maybe her newfound concerns about Leland were the product of an adrenaline crash and too little sleep. If that was the case, then she would owe him a huge apology.

But not now.

Not until she was sure.

"You need to be careful of Darrin," Leland said, not to her but rather to Jax. "He's fighting a civil lawsuit filed by the woman he raped. The DNA that Paige gathered at the crime scene is admissible in that particular trial, and Darrin wants Paige to admit she lied and planted evidence."

She'd known about the civil suit, of course, but with everything else going on, she hadn't mentioned it to Jax. Of course, Darrin already had a motive to come after her—revenge—but this only added to it. Maybe he believed if he killed her, or drove her crazy, then she wouldn't be able to testify at the trial. Or be around to try to get him convicted of the original charges.

"Did you come to my house yesterday?" Jax asked Leland. "Did you break in?"

Leland huffed, clearly insulted, and tapped his badge. "I uphold the law. I don't break it." Another huff. "Look, obviously you have a beef with me because Paige turned to me and not to you after she was nearly killed, but I'm not the enemy here. Paige and I have a history together, and she trusted me. Not you."

Now it was Jax who was insulted. Or maybe just riled. "Paige turned to you because she thought that was the only way to save our son. It wasn't."

"Maybe. But the danger's still here, isn't it? Your son is at risk, and that didn't happen until Paige came back."

She hadn't exactly had a choice about that, either. "The Moonlight Strangler found me," she reminded Leland, though there was no way he could have forgotten something as monumental as that.

Still, Leland shook his head. "I went to your apartment in Houston yesterday, looking for you. When you weren't there, I used my key to get in."

Jax jumped right on that. "He has a key?"

Paige nodded. Not her doing, exactly. "The apartment is in Leland's name. He got an extra key when he signed the lease."

Something she hadn't known about until weeks after she'd moved in, and Leland had surprised her one morning. After that, Paige had installed a swinging door bar latch and used it anytime she was inside.

Leland nodded. "When I was there yesterday, I found a listening device in the kitchen. Someone must have broken in and planted it there."

With everything else that had gone on, that shouldn't have chilled her to the bone. But it did. Someone had spied on her. And still was, judging from the texts she'd gotten.

"The bug had been there a while," Leland went on, "because there was some dust on it. My theory is that Darrin found you, broke in and planted the bug."

Jax lifted his shoulder. "If Darrin knew where she was, why not just go after her and confront her?"

Yet another chilling thought.

"Because I think Darrin wants to torment her first," Leland continued. "Over the past months, Paige and I talked a lot. About her life. About the attack. I think that's how Darrin found out the details of the attack that hadn't been released to the press. And I believe he used those details to set up that meeting yesterday. The one that nearly got Paige killed—again."

Paige looked at Jax, but he wasn't dismissing any of this. Neither was she. As sickening as it was to think Darrin might have tried to kill her, it was also somewhat of a relief. Because it would mean the Moonlight Strangler might not be after her.

"Paige's apartment needs to be thoroughly searched," Jax insisted. "Any computers she used, as well."

Leland nodded. "I'm working on it. I've also arranged a safe house for Paige." His gaze shifted back to her. "And I'd like you to go there with me now. Before you say no, just think it through. If you're away from the Crockett ranch, your son will be safe."

If only that were true.

However, Jax might believe that. He might want to send her far, far away. But just the thought of it crushed her heart. She'd barely gotten to spend any time with Matthew, and now she might have to leave.

Or not.

The look Jax shot Leland could have frozen the Sahara. "Paige isn't going anywhere with you."

She hadn't even realized she was holding her breath until it rushed out. But Jax obviously wasn't feeling any relief. It was a mix of anger and frustration. Some of it aimed at Leland. Some at her. The rest, at himself.

"You think that's wise?" Leland pressed. "You said someone had broken into your house. That someone could have planted a bug like the one in her apartment. Paige shouldn't be here until there's been a thorough sweep. She could stay at the safe house until you're sure everything is clean here."

"Paige isn't going with you," Jax said again, without hesitation. "I'm making arrangements for a place for Matthew and her, and I'll be the one to take them there."

Maybe he truly believed Leland could be the bad guy in all of this, or maybe Jax just didn't trust the man because Leland had helped her fake her death. Either way, Leland's safe house was out.

Thank God.

"You need to go to the sheriff's office," Jax reminded Leland. Without holstering his gun, Levi returned from talking to the ranch hands and came onto the porch with Jax and her. And he hurried, too. "My brother needs to ask you some questions."

"Because you Crocketts think I'm dirty," Leland snarled. "I'm not. And I can't help it if you're jealous of me and your ex-wife." He put a lot of emphasis on the words *jealous* and *ex*.

Words that caused Jax's eyes to narrow, but that still didn't stop him from getting to her. "If you're waiting for me to thank you for not telling me that Paige was alive, you'll be waiting an eternity."

Leland stood there, looking at her, no doubt waiting for her to agree to go with him. But Paige only shook her head.

"I'm sorry," she said.

With all the harsh words and glares that'd gone on in the past ten minutes, her generic apology seemed to bother Leland the most. He looked down at the ground a moment and mumbled something she didn't catch before he turned and headed back to his truck.

Jax didn't even wait until Leland had driven away before he turned to Levi. "Get Chase and Matthew out here. We all need to leave right now. Leland was right about one thing. Whoever's behind this could have planted a bug. Or something worse."

"Worse?" Levi asked.

Jax grabbed the keys for the cruiser. "There could be a bomb."

Chapter Nine

Jax wasn't sure if this was the right thing to do, but he didn't want to risk keeping Matthew in their home even a second longer.

He wanted to kick himself for not considering sooner that the killer—or rather the would-be killer—could have set a second bomb. One that would blow up the house and kill them all.

"Are you sure this is a good idea?" Paige asked when Jax pulled the cruiser to a stop in front of the main ranch house. His family's home.

She was eyeing the place as if it were the lion's den. And considering how much his family disliked her, in a way it was. Still, he didn't have a lot of options at the moment. He'd had to move fast to get Matthew, Paige and his brothers away from his house, and he needed to regroup.

"We won't be here long," he assured her.

And hoped that was true.

Since Chase had called ahead with a warning of their arrival and the reason for it, his mother, Iris, was already in the door, frantically motioning for them to come in. Jax got them moving, fast, so they wouldn't be out in the open any longer than necessary. Chase had Matthew bundled in his arms, and they hurried up the steps, his mother maneuvering them all inside. The moment they were all in, she locked the door and set the security alarm.

"Are you all right?" his mother asked, her attention landing on each of them before it settled on Paige. His mom made a face, but Jax didn't think it was solely of disapproval but had more to do with Paige's bruises and stitches.

"We're fine," Jax lied. Paige mumbled something similar.

At least the tension and fear weren't bothering Matthew. He grinned when he saw his grandmother and reached for her. Iris took him into her arms right away and kissed him.

"Paige," his mother said. Sort of a greeting, but there was no welcome-back in her tone. Nor her eyes.

"Iris," Paige answered. And her discomfort came through loud and clear even though her voice was a hoarse whisper. "Thank you for allowing me to be here."

Right. He figured Paige wasn't nearly as thankful as she was just glad to be out of a place that might have a bomb in it.

The silence settled in. Thick and uncomfortable before Jax did something about it. After all, it wasn't as if there weren't things to do.

"I didn't bring any of Matthew's clothes or toys,"

Jax explained to his mother. "I'll need to change him out of those jammies."

"I'll do it," she offered. "He has plenty of extra clothes here. And I'm sure we can find some toys." She winked at her grandson.

Jax was sure of that, too, since Matthew often stayed the night with his grandmother, Aunt Addie and Addie's husband, Weston, who all lived in the house. Matthew had been especially eager to do that since Addie had given birth to her son, Daniel. Even though Daniel was still way too young to actually play with Matthew, Matthew enjoyed being around him. It also helped that Addie and his mom spoiled him and had a huge playroom filled with every kind of toy a kid could ever want.

"Mommy," Matthew said, and he pointed to Paige. "Her home."

"Yes, I can see that." Iris managed a smile. Not a genuine one, of course, but it seemed to make Matthew happy.

"Cookie?" Matthew asked his grandmother.

Despite the mess they were in, Jax had to smile. His son already knew the perks of coming to Grandma's house.

"It's a little too early for a cookie," Iris explained, "but maybe after I've changed your clothes and you've had your breakfast. Are you hungry?"

Matthew nodded, but his mischievous grin let Jax know that the kid was still hoping for that cookie. And would likely get one.

Iris glanced at Paige, then Jax. "You can get Paige settled into one of the guest rooms. I'll go ahead and take care of Matthew."

Jax wasn't sure they'd be there long enough for Paige to need a guest room, but she might want a place to escape while he was making plans to get them to a safe location.

"I'll have the cruiser searched," Chase volunteered when his mother left with Matthew.

"Thanks. But don't search the house just yet. I want the bomb squad to go through it first."

Chase made a sound of agreement. "I'll call and get as many people out here as possible to look for those cameras."

Yeah, because until that was cleared up, Jax couldn't take Paige and Matthew to the safe house. It was a call that Jax could have made himself, but after one look at Paige, he figured that the guest room wasn't just optional. She needed it.

"I should have apologized to your mother," she said when Chase stepped away. "Not that it would have done any good."

It wouldn't have. Iris had taken it hard when Paige and he divorced. Had taken it even harder when she thought Paige had been murdered. It would be difficult to undo all that grief and hurt. Still, it would have to happen. He had to believe they'd catch the person behind the attacks and move on with their lives.

Eventually.

And that meant somehow he had to come to terms

with the fact that Paige would want partial custody of Matthew. She'd want to be his mother. But that was a worry for a different time.

Jax led her to the first guest room, only to remember it'd once been his room. A room where Paige and he had made out when they'd been in high school. No sex here. That'd happened later after they'd hooked up when she had come home from college. Still, those make-out memories seemed to be still lingering around.

Of course, his body egged those memories on.

Jax wasn't sure if Paige remembered their time together here, mainly because she dodged his gaze when they walked in. However, when the gaze-dodging ended, he saw plenty in the quick glance she gave him.

"I'll just freshen up." She fluttered her fingers toward the bathroom. "And then I can come down and help you with any arrangements that need to be made. I can spend some time with Matthew, too."

He certainly couldn't fault her for wanting to do that. She loved their son as much as Jax did. That's why this hurt so much.

"Am I responsible for that?" she asked. She touched the center of his forehead, which was bunched up.

"Yeah," he admitted. Probably shouldn't have, though. Because his bunched-up forehead was from worry about a subject he should probably wait until later to discuss with her. But his body had a different notion about that, too.

"I'm not used to sharing Matthew," he admitted.

Which didn't make sense. Jax shared him all the time with his family. Still, this was different.

"I understand." And that's all Paige said for several moments. "Just know that I won't interfere with the life you've made for him. Or the life you've made for yourself. I'll just figure out a way to fit into it."

The words were right. Heck, they were probably even true. For now, anyway. But soon, once the danger had passed, Paige would want more. She'd want to be a mother to her son.

She stepped away but then stopped, touching her fingers to her stitches. "You think you can get me some aspirin or maybe even something stronger?"

"Sure. How bad is the pain?" Something he should have already asked. Not just for the stitches but for her other scrapes and bruises, as well.

"Not bad."

Probably a lie. Definitely a lie, he amended, when he looked into her eyes. Yep, there it was. The pain, the fear…everything.

Everything.

Including the old attraction.

It was like a dangerous, hot powder keg sitting in the room. Something that should have had him moving away so he could get her some pain meds. But he didn't move. Not away from her, anyway.

Jax moved toward her, and while he was still in mid-step, he slid his hand around the back of her neck and pulled her to him. No resistance. None. In fact, it was

Paige who upped the ante by putting her mouth to his. He did something about that, fast.

He kissed right back.

Oh, man. There it was, that powder keg going off in his head.

The heat, fire and taste of her roared through him, and it only took a second for him to want not only this but a whole lot more.

She moved into the kiss when he deepened it and took hold of his arms. Anchoring him. Unless she thought he was about to run off. He wasn't. Jax stayed there, body to body with her, and kissed her until he couldn't stand the ache any more. Only then did he move back.

And he instantly felt his body urging him to return.

Paige's breath was gusting now. His wasn't exactly level, either, and they stood there staring at each other. Maybe waiting for the other to admit that had been a stupid mistake. Playing with fire, and they could both get burned.

Matthew, too.

Because that kind of mistake could cause Jax to lose focus.

"Well, at least I don't need the pain meds now," she said, and before he could think of a smart-ass comeback, she headed to the bathroom. "Let me wash my face, and we'll go back downstairs."

She paused only a second to glance in the direction of the bed. He doubted she was in any shape for sex, but whenever they were near each other, sex came up.

Paige nixed the sex and did indeed go into the bathroom. Jax thought this might be a good time to ram his head against the wall. He might just knock some sense into himself. However, that thought disappeared when he heard something he didn't want to hear. A voice coming from downstairs.

Cord.

Oh, joy. Just what he didn't need, another run-in with what had to be the surliest DEA agent in the country. Of course, it didn't help that Cord had been the one to help Paige keep her death a secret. Soon, Jax wanted to have a discussion about that.

When Paige came out of the bathroom, she must have noticed his change in expression, but she must have also heard Cord's voice because she hurried past him and went downstairs. Cord was still at the door, talking with Chase, but that ended when he spotted Paige.

"I think we have a problem," Cord said, snagging her gaze and moving closer to her.

"He's been analyzing Paige's phone records and text messages," Chase relayed, and he sounded as unhappy as Jax was about having Cord part of his investigation.

Of course, Chase probably didn't have the same motivation as Jax for that particular unhappiness. Chase just wouldn't like having a renegade lawman who operated with plenty of shades of gray. Jax didn't like it that Cord had formed this *bond* with Paige. The last time Paige had teamed up with someone to catch the serial killer, she'd nearly died.

The same could happen this time.

And this time, the danger could pose a threat to Matthew.

Even though he already knew that, Jax let that thought settle in his mind. It didn't settle well. And this time not just because of Matthew but because of Paige herself.

Damn.

This was about that kiss.

He'd known from the start that it was a stupid thing to do, and now it was playing into his mind-set. Not good. Because the only mind-set he needed right now was to protect his little boy.

Chase locked the door, reset the security system, but he continued to keep watch out the side windows.

"I don't think any of those messages yesterday came from the Moonlight Strangler," Cord continued, his attention on Paige. "I've gone through every word, and it's just not the same as the other messages he sent earlier to you. Something's off."

Paige nodded. And groaned softly. "We have suspects. Two of them—Darrin Pittman and Leland Fountain. My money's on Darrin."

So was Jax's. But there was another possibility. "Maybe the Moonlight Strangler purposely altered the wording. He likes to play games. Likes to torment Paige. Maybe he wants her to believe she's got more than one person gunning for her."

"Cord," someone said before he had a chance to respond to that.

Addie, Jax's sister. Cord's sister, too, Jax had to remind himself. His parents had adopted Addie when she was three, the same age Jax had been at the time, and to him she'd always be his sister.

Addie went to Cord, hugged him and then turned to Paige to do the same thing. Paige went a little stiff, no doubt from surprise, but she stiffened even more when Levi's fiancée, Alexa Dearborn, came into the foyer.

The tension suddenly got a whole lot thicker.

Jax braced himself for Alexa to lash out at Paige. After all, they'd been best friends, and Alexa had blamed herself for getting Paige killed. But Paige wasn't dead, and that meant Alexa had grieved for nothing.

But there was no lashing out.

The breath Alexa took was one of relief, and she hurried to Paige to hug her, too. No relief for Paige, though. Jax was watching her and saw the guilt in her eyes. The fear, too. Because while Alexa and the rest of them had lived with Paige's so-called death, her return had put them all in danger.

"I wish I'd been able to let you know," Paige said.

"I'm just glad you're home," Alexa assured her. She volleyed some glances between Paige and him. "Are you two back together?"

"No," Paige blurted out. It was certainly a fast enough response. Adamant enough, too. But it didn't exactly ring true.

That kiss again.

It'd screwed up a lot of things, but mainly Jax's head.

He wanted to believe it wouldn't happen again, but he didn't even try to lie to himself about it. That attraction wasn't going away, so the best solution was to try to keep some distance between Paige and him. That wasn't going to happen, though, either, until this danger had passed.

Alexa lightly touched her fingers to the crescent-shaped scar on Paige's cheek. It wasn't as pronounced as the recent bruises and stitches, but it would be a life-long reminder of just how close she had really come to dying.

"We need to catch that monster." Alexa's voice was barely a whisper, but it came through loud and clear.

Cord was the first to nod, though they all agreed. "We have to figure out for sure if there are any other players in this," Cord added. "I personally don't think the Moonlight Strangler would have partnered with anyone else to go after Paige. He's had no trouble killing women on his own."

Like the scar, it was yet another brutal reminder. And the truth.

"Also, the Moonlight Strangler's never used explosives at any of his crime scenes," Jax added. "My bet's on Darrin, too. He's got the money and motive to pull off something like this."

"Come on." Addie slipped her arm around Paige's waist. "You can take a quick break from the investigation so we can catch up. I want you to meet my husband and our son, and you can have breakfast with Matthew."

Jax gave his sister a *thank-you* look. Paige did need

time to catch her breath. Needed time with Matthew, too. However, Paige had barely managed a step when Jax's phone buzzed.

"Jericho," he said, looking at the screen.

That stopped Paige, of course. It stopped everyone, because Jericho was interviewing both their suspects right about now, and he might have gotten a break in the case.

"Good news, I hope," Jax said when he answered the call and put it on speaker.

"I'm not sure what kind of news it is right now. A package arrived for Paige here at the sheriff's office. A courier service delivered it, and I had it checked for explosives. There aren't any."

That got Jax's attention. Paige's, too. "A package?" she repeated. "Who sent it and what's in it?"

"Don't know who sent it, but there were just two things inside. A cell phone and a typed note telling Paige to call the number programmed into it. Only Paige. The note said if anyone else called, there'd be no answer."

Jericho blew out a long breath that was audible even from the other end of the line. "Jax, I think you should bring Paige in right away. Not just to deal with the phone. But I think she should talk to the courier. He says he's got orders to speak to only her."

Chapter Ten

Paige tried to steady her heart rate. Tried not to think the worst. But since the *worst* seemed to be the norm for her, it was hard not to wonder if this package was some kind of ruse to draw her out.

Still, she didn't have a lot of options—also the norm for her lately—because she hadn't wanted Jericho to bring the courier to the ranch, yet she wanted any answers the man might be able to give.

"Please tell me Matthew will be all right," she said when Jax pulled the cruiser not in the parking lot of the sheriff's office but directly in front of it. Of course, she knew what he would say.

Matthew was safe.

And it was as true as it could be. Chase, Levi and Weston were all there. Cord, too. Plus, there were at least a half dozen armed ranch hands. In addition to that, both Chase and Levi had searched the cruiser to make sure it wasn't bugged or that a tracking device hadn't been attached. It was clear. However, that didn't mean someone wasn't in town watching the sheriff's office and waiting for them to arrive.

"It's not Matthew I'm worried about right now." Jax glanced around the area as if he expected them to be attacked again.

And they very well could be.

Because this could be a ruse not to go after Matthew, but rather to go after Jax and her.

Jericho must have thought it was possible, too, because he had suggested that Levi or Chase drive in with them so they'd have backup. But Jax and she had wanted that backup at the ranch. Something they'd easily agreed on. At least they were on the same page when it came to their son's safety.

Paige mentally shrugged.

Apparently on the same page when it came to that kiss, too. Jax had hardly looked at her since then, and that was a good thing. Kissing was a distraction, and it muddied waters that she needed to be clear right now. All their focus had to be on protecting Matthew.

Jax drew his gun, and with his body practically wrapped around her, he hurried her into the building. Her hair was still damp from the shower she'd hurriedly taken. Not exactly a luxury. She hadn't managed to take one the night before, and she had to wash off some of the scents from the attack. Also, she'd needed all the help she could get loosening up her tight muscles. So tight that her neck was stiff.

The moment they got inside the sheriff's office, Paige spotted Mack, Jericho and a tall, thin man with dark hair. The courier, no doubt. He looked even more nervous about this than Paige did. His Adam's apple was bobbing, and his eyes were darting all around.

There was no sign of Leland or Darrin, so maybe that meant Jericho had finished with them. Or maybe they were still being interviewed by one of the deputies.

"His name is Chad Farmer," Jericho supplied, tipping his head to the man.

Jax's brother was seated at a desk, leaning back in the chair. Almost casually. But there was nothing casual about that dangerous look Jericho was giving their visitor.

"Does he have a record?" Jax asked.

"Not yet. But he knows he's going to jail after he talks to you. I'm charging him with obstruction of justice for not answering my questions. Oh, and for having a broken taillight on his car. And I'll tack on anything else I can think to charge him with."

Evidently, Jericho wasn't pleased with this courier. Well, neither was Paige.

She went closer to the desk and looked in the box that was next to Jericho. Only the typed note and the phone, just as Jericho had said.

"No prints," Jericho told her. "Well, other than the prints belonging to this clown, and his are the only ones on the outside of the box."

"The man who hired me said he'd kill me if I talked to anyone but you," Chad volunteered, his attention on her.

"Well, I'm here now, so talk," she demanded. "Who was he?"

Chad immediately shook his head. "He didn't say, and I didn't get a good look at him. He was in the backseat of my car when I got in it and put a gun to my head. He said I was to bring the box here and ask to speak to you. Only you. And if I said anything else to anyone I was a dead man."

Paige had no idea if any of this was true, but she could practically smell the fear on Chad. See it in his eyes, too.

"Did this man have an accent?" Paige pressed. "Was there anything about him that stood out?"

He shook his head to both questions. "He just said he'd know if I talked to anyone but you and that he'd make sure I was dead by morning if I did." Chad swallowed hard when he glanced at Jericho. "Will you ask the sheriff if he's really going to arrest me?"

"You bet I am." Jericho motioned to Mack. "Lock him up and hold him until I can find out if he's telling the truth. If he's not, I can add another charge to the ones I already have."

Chad opened his mouth and seemed ready to argue about that, but he looked at the window, his gaze shifting over the sidewalk and buildings. "He could be watching," Chad said to Paige. "Tell the sheriff to go ahead and put me in jail. Just make sure someone's guarding me so he can't get to me."

Well, that worked in Chad's favor. He was willing to be in jail rather than speak to anyone else. Either he was truly innocent or else he was playing them for some reason she couldn't figure out. Either way,

Paige was glad when Mack led the man toward the holding cell.

"It's been a busy morning for all of us," Jericho said, pushing the box closer for her to see. "I still have Darrin in the interview room. Last I checked he was playing a game on his phone, but I've been too tied up with this to talk to him. Dexter's in there with him now."

"I'm surprised Darrin didn't bring one of his attorneys with him," Jax remarked.

"Oh, he called them all right. They're on the way. A whole team of them, apparently. And they're going to sue me for harassment. I don't think Darrin liked it much when I wasn't bothered about that."

No, he wouldn't have liked that. Darrin loved to intimidate people. That didn't work so well on the Crocketts, though. They had just as much money as he did—possibly more. And they had badges. Darrin wasn't big on dealing with authority figures.

"What about Leland?" she asked.

Jericho shook his head. "He hasn't come in. If he's not here by the time we've figured out exactly what this box means, I'll give him a call. Or better yet, call his lieutenant."

That wouldn't please Leland, but Paige couldn't worry about hurting his feelings. She had to get the truth.

The truth that might be in that box.

She took out the note, trying not to touch anything but the edges. Jericho had already said it didn't have prints on it, but touching it seemed like touching the killer. Because she figured whoever wanted her dead had to be behind this.

"'Paige,'" she read aloud from the note, "'this phone and mine are burners, and if I don't hear your sweet voice when it rings, then I hang up, and you'll lose your chance to speak to me. Wouldn't want that, would you? Call me right now. The number's programmed in already.'"

"It's a burner," Jericho verified. "No way to trace it."

Exactly what she'd expected. And Paige knew what she had to do next. She had to talk to this monster and figure out who he was and how to stop him.

"Ready?" Jericho asked her. He took out a recorder, and when she nodded, he pressed the button.

Her hands were shaking, but she didn't realize how much until Jax reached over and touched the number in the contacts. It rang. And rang. By the fourth ring, her heart was in her throat, and she was afraid all of this had been a sick hoax.

But then someone answered. Whoever it was didn't say a word, no doubt waiting to hear her "sweet voice."

"It's me," she said, trying to sound strong. She failed.

"Paige," the man answered. "Good girl, following orders. I knew you wouldn't want to miss this chance for us to chat."

The chill went through her, head to toe, and if she hadn't sat down in the chair, she would have fallen.

"It's him." She had to clear her throat and repeat it for her words to have any sound. "It's the Moonlight Strangler. I recognize the voice."

"Well, of course you do, sweetheart," he purred. "We had some time to talk last year."

That gave her some steel that she seriously needed. "Yes, while you were cutting my face."

"Yes, that. A nasty obsession of mine. We bad boys do have our bad ways, don't we?"

Because Jax's hand was on her shoulder—she wasn't even sure when he'd put it there, though—she could feel his muscles tense. See Jericho's doing the same. Paige could tell they both wanted to speak up, badly, to blast this monster to smithereens, but if they said anything, the killer might end the call.

That couldn't happen.

Just talking to him made her want to throw up, but she had to do this.

"How did you find out I was alive?" she asked.

"I have my ways, but I will say, you had me fooled. I really thought you were number thirty-one."

The FBI didn't have a confirmed number of bodies they could attribute to the Moonlight Strangler, so she didn't know if that was true or not.

"How did you know I was alive?" she pressed. She prayed her voice wouldn't freeze up and that she could get through this without breaking down. God, she could feel his knife cutting into her.

"I heard about the attack at the Crockett ranch," he said. "That's when I found out."

She jumped right on that. "It wasn't you behind that attack?"

"No way." He sounded insulted. "That's not my style. Too sloppy. Too many working parts. But someone wanted to make you think it was me. Someone using my name and reputation. I don't like that. I kill people who pretend to be me."

That time, he sounded dangerous. Not that she'd needed to hear it to know it. The proof was on her face. Plus, he'd actually murdered another man when he had tried to make everyone believe that the Moonlight Strangler was after Alexa.

"So, if it wasn't you last night," she continued, "who was it?"

"That sounds like a personal problem. Yours, not mine. Use all those cowboy cops you surround yourself with to figure it out. I just don't want to be blamed for something I haven't done. Yet."

The *yet* felt like a punch to the gut.

"Are you going to try to come after me again?" Paige wasn't sure, though, that she actually wanted to hear the answer.

"All in due time. I've always wanted to do this mother-daughter thing, and you're my chance to make that happen. But I have someone else in my sights right now. Oh, she's such a sweet little thing. A blonde, like you. I'll bet she begs for mercy when I cut her. I like it when they beg."

That was it. He ended the call before Paige could scream for him to stop. The flashbacks came at her full force. All of them at once. The sounds. The pain. His voice. And now he was going to do that to someone else.

"You have to stop him," she begged, though she knew there was nothing they could do. The only way she could save her sanity was to believe it'd been all talk, that he wasn't about to add another victim to his list.

But she knew in her heart that soon, very soon, they'd hear the news of another murder. Another one that she hadn't been able to stop.

"I would ask if you're okay," Jericho grumbled when he hit the button to end the recording, "but I know you're not." He went to the water cooler, got her a cup and brought it back to her.

Even though she wasn't much of a drinker, Paige wished it was something stronger. She downed the whole cup, but her throat was still bone dry.

Mack came back into the room, and even though he looked at her, he didn't ask what'd happened. Good thing. Because Paige wasn't sure she could tell him that it felt as if she'd just been crushed by an avalanche.

Jericho eased away from her so that Jax could step in. Not exactly a subtle move, and the brothers exchanged a long glance before Jericho went to another desk to make a call.

"He'll kill this woman," she managed to say, "and come after me again."

"No, he won't, because we'll stop him."

Jax sounded so sure of that, but Paige didn't actually feel that certainty, that promise, until he pulled her into his arms. Just the simple gesture gave her a lot more comfort than it should.

"Come on," Jax said, helping her to her feet. "I'll take you back to the ranch. Holding Matthew should help."

It would, but she shook her head. "I don't want to lead the Moonlight Strangler to the ranch."

"He already knows where the ranch is. He knows someone you care about will be there. And we've got people in place to make sure he doesn't come anywhere near you."

Paige knew that no measures of security were foolproof. Especially when it came to this particular killer. But Jax was right about one thing—holding Matthew would make her feel better.

However, they hadn't even moved toward the door when Jericho held up his finger in a wait-a-minute gesture. "Don't touch it. Have Levi bag it and bring it in," he told the person he was speaking to, and he finished the call.

"Bag what?" Jax immediately asked.

"There don't appear to be any bombs at your place, but one of the ranch hands found a camera. It was attached to the bottom of the porch swing, and it appears to have some kind of listening device connected to it."

Jax cursed, shook his head. "That would have given the person a view of the yard, driveway and anyone coming in and out of the house. And the person would have been able to hear whatever we said when we were out there."

Yes, and as sickening as that was, at least it was better than a bomb. "When it's analyzed, we might be able to tell who was on the receiving end of the camera feed. Might." It was a long shot, though.

"There appears to be a print on the camera," Jericho added. "That's why I didn't want him to touch it."

She hated to get up her hopes, but this could be the break they were looking for. Well, unless it was just the prints of another hired gun. Still, that particular lackey might still be alive so they could question him.

Paige heard the sound of the front door opening, but she didn't actually get to see who was coming in. That's because Jax hooked his arm around her, maneuvering her behind him. Only then did she get a glimpse of their visitor.

Leland.

He'd finally arrived for his interview. And he wasn't alone. He was holding on to a very distraught-looking Belinda. She was sobbing and leaning against him. She didn't appear to be hurt, but her face was sweaty and red, and her hair was disheveled.

What had happened now?

And why were those two together?

Belinda immediately left Leland and made a beeline for Jax. She flung herself at him, landing in his arms.

"Someone broke into my house," she said through the sobs. Her words rushed together. "I didn't know he was there, but he must have been watching me."

"Slow down," Jax told her. He helped her to one of the chairs and had her sit. Jericho did water duty again and got her a cup.

While Belinda was drinking that, Paige turned to Leland. "What happened?"

He lifted his shoulder. "I don't know. I pulled into the parking lot and I saw her crying and stumbling. I helped her in." Leland didn't actually look at Belinda. He kept his attention on Paige. "She's your son's nanny, right?"

Paige nodded. Matthew's nanny and Jax's friend. A friend who wanted to be a lot more. Paige got a reminder of that when Belinda lunged at Jax and went right back into his arms.

"You have to help me," Belinda begged.

"I will. Now tell me what happened."

Belinda's tears didn't exactly dry up when she looked at Paige, but she frowned as if she didn't want Paige around for this.

"I could wait in one of the interview rooms while you talk to her," Paige suggested, not to Belinda but to Jax.

He nixed that right away with a head shake and moved out of Belinda's arms again. "Darrin's back there. Stay here where I can keep an eye on you."

Oh, Belinda did not like that, and Paige got a nasty glare from the woman. That alone was enough reason for Paige to stay put. Plus, she really didn't want to be any closer to Darrin.

"Did you see the person who broke in?" Jax asked Belinda. His tone wasn't impatient exactly, but it was close. Probably because it was still morning and they'd already been through the wringer a couple of times.

Belinda took her time gathering her breath. "I didn't see him, but I heard his phone ring. And then I heard him talking. I ran straight here."

Jax and she exchanged glances with Jericho. It was Jericho who continued. "How long ago did this happen?"

"Fifteen or so minutes."

Mercy. That was about the same time Paige had called the Moonlight Strangler. Was it possible he'd been there in Belinda's house?

"Did you hear anything the intruder said?" Paige pressed.

Belinda shook her head, then she stopped. "I did. I didn't remember it until now, but I did hear something." She looked at Paige, her eyes suddenly narrowing. "He said your name."

Oh, God. That's the first thing the killer had said when he answered the phone. *Paige.* And that could only mean one thing.

Belinda was the Moonlight Strangler's next target.

Chapter Eleven

Hell.

Jax wanted to dismiss all this as a really bad coincidence. But he couldn't. The Moonlight Strangler had admitted he had another woman on his radar. A blonde.

Like Belinda.

And Jax wouldn't put it past the killer to go after yet someone else close to his family.

"What is it?" Belinda asked, obviously picking up on the bad vibes.

Jax wasn't sure how much he should tell her. This could all be part of the killer's sick game, a ruse. Or Belinda could be lying to get some attention from him. But he couldn't take that chance.

"The Moonlight Strangler could have been the person in your house."

Belinda's breath rushed out, and she looked ready to keel over. All right. That reaction looked pretty darn genuine.

"You're responsible for this," Belinda muttered several moments later. And she was looking at Paige when she said it.

"How is Paige responsible?" Jax asked, huffing. But Paige wasn't huffing. She was a little thunderstruck.

"She drew him here." Belinda made it seem as if the answer was obvious. Her anger was plenty obvious, as well. "He knew Paige was alive. He must have seen her like I did."

Belinda froze, and her hand flew to her mouth. Jax got a really bad feeling that Belinda wasn't talking about having seen Paige the day before.

"How long have you known I was alive?" Paige demanded, and it was a demand. Jax wanted to know the same thing.

Belinda glanced around, swallowed hard. "Two weeks. But I wasn't sure it was her. I only suspected."

Jax had to get his teeth unclenched. "And you didn't tell me?"

"I said I didn't know for sure, and I didn't want you to, well, get your hopes up or anything." Belinda looked everywhere but at him. Her attention finally settled on Paige. "I bought this facial recognition software. I had a feeling in my gut you were still alive, so I started doing internet searches. The software matched your face to a photo that someone had taken at a store opening in Houston."

Jax turned to Paige to see if that could have happened. And she nodded. "A toy store. But I didn't know they'd taken my picture. I arrived there just as they were doing the ribbon cutting, and I guess I got in the shot."

"Why were you there?" Leland asked.

"To buy Matthew something. I was going to have Cord give it to him, but Cord wasn't going to say it was from me."

A toy.

Damn.

"I wasn't sure it was her," Belinda repeated.

Yeah, she had been. Jax could see it in her eyes. Belinda hadn't wanted him to know that Paige was alive because he would have gone after her and found her so she could give him answers.

Now he had those answers, but they weren't ones that Jax liked.

"I know this is a lot to take in," Leland said, "but it sounds as if Belinda could be in real danger."

Jax could add another "yeah" to that, too.

"Belinda can't go back to your place," Paige insisted at the same moment Jericho turned to Mack.

"Why don't you take Belinda to the break room and have her give you a statement. I'll have Dexter go out to her house and look around."

"Someone needs to go with Dexter," Paige blurted out. "He might need backup."

Jericho nodded, but since he was taking out his phone, he'd already considered that possibility. "I'll call in one of the reserve deputies."

"Find that man," Belinda said. To Jericho. "And arrest him."

"If he's still there, Dexter will find him," Jax told her. But he seriously doubted the Moonlight Strangler would be hanging around waiting for the cops to show up.

Belinda caught on to Jax's hand when Mack tried to lead her to the break room. "Jax, I want you to take my statement. I want you to wait with me. Please."

Jax wasn't immune to the fear she was no doubt feeling, but he had to shake his head. "I can't stay." It wasn't safe for Paige to be here, and he didn't want to be away from Matthew any longer. "But Mack will take good care of you."

Belinda looked as if he'd slapped her. And then Jax saw the shock morph to hurt. Then, a glare. Maybe even hatred.

The hatred wasn't aimed at him but at Paige.

Okay, that helped with the guilt he was feeling over not staying there with her. What was going on? Was this just a case of jealousy or something more? He hoped like the devil that Belinda hadn't made some kind of contact with the Moonlight Strangler so that the killer would go after Paige.

"I've been good to you," Belinda added, still sounding more angry than hurt.

He didn't respond, though Belinda was obviously waiting for something. But Jax wasn't sure what to say. He was emotionally spent right now, and he needed to focus his mind and energies elsewhere. Later, if it turned out that Belinda was completely innocent in all of this, then he would owe her an apology.

Belinda didn't put up a fuss when Mack led her up the hall, but she managed to work in one last hard look at Paige.

Jax immediately turned to Leland. "You were supposed to come in a couple of hours ago. Where were you?"

Yet another glare, and it was Jax who got a dose of it this time. "I had work to do." He tapped his badge that was clipped to his belt. "I'm a cop, remember."

"You're also a suspect in the attack last night."

Judging from the sound of surprise Paige made, she hadn't expected Jax to spell it out in no uncertain terms, but there it was. Jax didn't have time to sugarcoat it. And Leland didn't care for it one bit.

"The Moonlight Strangler was behind that," Leland insisted.

"Not according to him. Paige just got off the phone with him, and he said someone else is responsible. He's not very happy about someone using his name, either. He murdered the last person who tried to do that."

Leland had no doubt heard all about it, but it still took a moment for it to sink in. Or maybe it just took him some time to realize that Jax had just told him that he might be on the killer's list, too.

However, Leland didn't respond to Jax. He turned to Paige. "Your ex has already turned you against me." It wasn't a question, and he didn't wait for Paige to say anything. He looked at Jericho. "Are you ready to do that interview?"

Jericho didn't usually look stressed, but he sure did now. He huffed, then hitched his thumb to the hall. "Wait in the second interview room on the right."

Jax waited until Leland was in the room before he

said anything to his brother. "I don't think Belinda has the resources to hire gunmen, but I'll check. I'll check on Leland, too."

Jericho nodded. "It doesn't always take money to hire thugs. Both of those gunmen had records. It's possible they owed favors to Leland or someone else." He paused, groaned softly as if very uncomfortable as to what he was about to say. "You didn't know Belinda was in love with you?"

Paige decided it was a good time to go to the water cooler and get another drink, but Jax didn't lower his voice. Because this was something she probably should hear.

"I knew," Jax admitted. "But I never led Belinda to believe she could be anything more than a friend and Matthew's nanny."

Jericho made a sound of agreement. "It's that pretty face of yours. Women just can't resist you." Jericho probably meant that as a joke, to help with the raw tension in the room. It didn't. But Jax was thankful for it, anyway.

"I don't think Belinda would have tried to hurt me," Jax went on. Hurting Paige, though, might be a different matter. Belinda could have been so distraught over hearing Paige was alive that she did something stupid.

Like convincing two men to scare Paige away by making her believe that the Moonlight Strangler was after her again and that her presence at the ranch put Matthew in danger.

However, the huge problem with that was the same

warning he'd given Leland. The Moonlight Strangler didn't care much for being used.

Jax was ready to try to get Paige out of there again, but he'd barely got her moving when he heard a door open in the hall. At first he thought he was going to have to go another round with Belinda.

But it was Darrin.

"Good news," he said. "You don't get sued today. We have to reschedule this little chat because my chief lawyer just called, and he's been involved in a car accident in San Antonio. He can't make it."

"You don't look broken up about that," Jericho remarked.

"I'm not. I fired him, of course, which means I'll need to get a new lawyer before you can grill me with your lies. Or rather *her* lies." He shot a glance at Paige before turning to Jax. "Besides, you don't have any grounds to hold me."

"Not yet," Jax warned him. "We're waiting on some lab results."

Maybe it was Jax's expression or his tone, but Darrin actually seemed to take notice.

"Lab results?" Darrin questioned. "Ones that Paige faked?"

"Paige had nothing to do with this. A cop found the evidence, and the crime lab is processing it." At least it soon would be once Levi brought it in. "Paige hasn't been near the lab."

Darrin's jaw tightened. "What did you find? Or what is it you *think* you found?"

No way would Jax tell him about the print on the camera, but it would make all this so much easier if the print turned out to be Darrin's. Or if a money trail for those hired guns led right back to him.

"You can go," Jericho said, not answering Darrin's question, either. "I'll call your lawyer when the lab results are back."

Darrin suddenly didn't seem to be in such a hurry to leave. He stood there, volleying glances at the three of them before he cursed and headed out. Jax went to the window to make sure he did indeed leave and that he didn't try to tamper with the cruiser.

"Don't let Belinda go back to her place," Jax said to Jericho. "I know we have a lot of manpower tied up, but—"

"Already taken care of," Jericho interrupted. "The other reserve deputy will put her in protective custody."

Good. He doubted Belinda would try to go back, anyway. Heck, she might never go back, but he didn't want to risk it. The Moonlight Strangler might have targeted Belinda simply because of her connection to Jax.

Jax waited until Darrin had driven away and his car was out of sight before he motioned for Paige to get moving. Every second outside was a huge risk, and he tried to minimize that by going out ahead of her to open the door. He practically stuffed her into the cruiser and then hurried to get behind the wheel. He drove off as fast as he could. However, he'd hardly pulled away from the station when his phone buzzed.

Chase.

Jax couldn't answer it fast enough.

"Matthew's fine," Chase said the moment he came on the line. "We all are. But a ranch hand spotted someone climbing over one of the fences." Chase paused. "The guy's armed with a rifle."

Even though he hadn't put the call on speaker, Paige must have heard what Chase said because she gasped. "Hurry," she told Jax, but he was already doing that.

"We've moved Mom and the others into the playroom, and Levi and the ranch hands are going after the guy."

"Paige and I are on our way back to the ranch," Jax let him know.

"Just be careful when you get here. The ranch hand said the rifle had a scope on it."

Which meant the shooter could go into sniper mode. He could set up cover behind one of the barns or trees and start shooting. Of course, the question was—who was his target? Someone inside the house? Or was it Paige and him?

"I'll call you when the situation's contained," Chase added before he hung up.

"The playroom?" Paige questioned the moment Jax was off the phone.

"It's safe, in the center of the house. We set it up a few months back after there was some trouble at the ranch."

It wasn't a panic room exactly, but there were no windows, and if someone did start shooting, the bullets would have to make it through multiple walls to hit anyone. Still, Jax wanted to be there to make sure this guy with the rifle didn't get inside. He didn't want a gunfight right on his family's doorstep.

Jax was already going well over the speed limit, but he pushed the accelerator even harder. Each minute felt like hours.

"We have to move Matthew to the safe house," Paige said.

No argument from him, and as soon as Jax was certain he could get them there safely, he would do it.

"Our security measures at the ranch worked. The ranch hand spotted the gunman," he reminded her. Reminded himself, too. But then Jax saw something he didn't want to see.

Smoke.

Not a small amount, either. It was thick and black and oozing over the road.

At first he thought someone had set a fire on the asphalt, and it took him a moment to realize it was coming from a house. Hell. It was the old Dawson place. A small house just off the road.

"Call the fire department," Jax said, tossing Paige his phone.

He eased up on the gas, not only because of the wall of smoke in front of him but because he needed to see if Herman Dawson had gotten out. The man was eighty if he was a day and a smoker. He could have set the place on fire.

But Jax knew this could be more than just an accidental fire. That's why he kept watch, or rather he tried to do that, when he slowed the cruiser to a crawl so he could have a better look. He prayed he'd see Herman in the yard, unharmed.

He didn't.

However, Jax did get a glimpse of a man near the blazing house. Not Herman, either. The man lifted a rifle and shot right into the cruiser.

SINCE PAIGE HAD her attention on the phone call she was making, she didn't see the shooter before the bullet blasted into the side window right next to her. The glass cracked and webbed, but the bullet didn't go through.

Thank God.

She didn't even have time to react to it before Jax took hold of her arm, unlatched her seat belt and pushed her down onto the floor. He didn't get down, though. He drew his gun, and in the same motion, he got them moving again.

Or at least that's what he tried to do.

But the shots started coming nonstop. Not just from the side. They came in front of them, too, directly from that wall of smoke.

Paige made the call to the fire department. Then she made one to Jericho and asked him to send someone immediately, but to approach with caution because of the shots being fired. Jax and she were only about ten minutes away from town, but it might take longer than that for Jericho to be able to make a safe approach.

And then Paige had a horrible thought.

What if there was an attack like this going on at the ranch?

She couldn't press Chase's number fast enough. But her heart crashed against her chest when he didn't answer.

Paige tried to assure herself that it was because he was in pursuit of that rifleman, but that person could have been a ruse to lure Levi and Chase out of the house so that someone could go after Matthew.

"Stay down," Jax warned her.

He didn't go forward, probably because he didn't know who was on the other side of the smoke. Maybe an entire team of hired killers. Instead, he threw the cruiser into reverse.

She did stay on the seat, but Paige also threw open the glove compartment and took out the gun that Jax had put there earlier before they'd started their drive to the sheriff's office. When he'd done that, he'd mumbled something about it just being a precaution.

Now she might have to use it to help save their lives and get them out of there so they could hurry to the ranch to protect their son.

Even though they were in the middle of cross fire, Paige felt the panic attack threaten. Not solely from this attack, though that was a huge part of it, but also just because she had a gun in her hand.

The flashbacks came.

Not of the Moonlight Strangler's attack. He hadn't used a gun. But from the attack that had left her parents dead. She'd witnessed it. Had been there to watch them both die, and even though it'd happened a long time ago, just holding the gun made those memories fresh and raw.

"Level your breathing," Jax said to her.

Only then did Paige realize her breaths were coming way too fast, and she was trembling. *Get a grip.* She'd worked her way through the panic attacks and didn't have time to deal with her old baggage. If she wanted to stay alive, she had to focus on the here and now.

Just as Jax was doing.

With his gaze volleying from the rear to the front of the cruiser, he kept them moving. Away from the fire and the gunmen. Paige only prayed they didn't have a wreck with any oncoming traffic. This was a farm road, but there were houses and other ranches all along it.

"Damn," Jax spat out.

She didn't have the time to ask why he'd said that. Paige quickly found out. When a bullet slammed into the back window of the cruiser. It was quickly followed by another one. Then, another.

Mercy.

They were being attacked on three sides, and while the cruiser was bullet resistant, it didn't mean those shots soon wouldn't get through. Plus, it seemed as if the gunmen were trying to shoot out the engine. If they managed that, Jax and she would be sitting ducks.

There was only one place for Jax to go. To the left. And that's the way he went. He jerked the steering wheel to the left, gunned the engine and the cruiser barreled off the road, crashing through a white wood fence and into a massive cornfield.

The cruiser bobbled and bounced on the uneven surface, the high stalks and the corn slapping against the car. The noise was practically deafening, but it didn't drown out the shots that continued to come at them.

The gunmen were either in pursuit or they had some of their buddies stashed in this cornfield. All in all, it wasn't a bad place to hide since she couldn't see anything except for corn stalks and the shattered glass in the windows.

Jax cursed when he hit a bad bump, and Paige's head collided with the dash. Right in the very spot where she had stitches. The pain shot through her so bad that she nearly lost her breath, but she had a huge incentive to regain it when the phone buzzed and she saw Chase's name on the screen.

"Is Matthew okay?" she asked, her words running together.

"Yes." Chase paused a heartbeat. "I didn't answer because I was on the line with Jericho. He's on his way out to you. Two of the hands are coming from the ranch."

"No, I want all the hands and you there with Matthew. This could be a trap."

"Maybe, but if so it didn't work. One of the hands shot the guy with the rifle, and there aren't any signs of another gunman."

Despite the nightmarish situation Jax and she were in, the relief came. She'd experience a thousand attacks aimed at her if these goons just kept her son out of it.

"Give him our location," Jax instructed.

She did. Well, as best she could. She'd driven by this cornfield hundreds of times over the years, but she had no idea just how much acreage was involved or what was even on the back side of it. There were plenty of ranch trails out here. Plus, there were no doubt rocks and such that could cause them to have a blowout.

"They're following us," she heard Jax say.

Paige stayed down, but she levered herself up just enough to see out the side window. She spotted the black SUV tearing through the cornfield behind them. The gunmen weren't leaning out of the windows. It wouldn't be safe enough for them to do that, but they'd no doubt be ready to resume this attack when they were out of the field.

Which happened a lot sooner than Paige expected.

The cruiser shot through the last row of corn, skidding onto what felt like gravel. Jax fought with the steering wheel, trying to regain control.

And Paige soon saw why he needed to do that.

There was a creek just to their right, and even though she couldn't see exactly where the water began, they seemed to be only a few inches from it.

It seemed to take an eternity for Jax to get control, and he managed to maneuver the cruiser away from the water. Barely in time. They likely wouldn't have drowned if the cruiser had gone in the creek, but it would have made it easy for the gunmen to kill them.

Once he was centered on the trail, Jax gunned the engine again, and Paige braced herself for more gunfire.

It didn't happen.

No shots at all. And that's why she wasn't sure why Jax cursed.

Paige looked in the mirror to see what was going on. The SUV wasn't following them. The driver was now on another trail, headed away from them.

She blew out a breath of relief. But it didn't last.

"Where does that trail lead?" she asked Jax. "Where are they going?"

A muscle flickered in his jaw. "To the ranch."

Chapter Twelve

It was hard to speed down a dirt and gravel trail that wasn't much wider than the cruiser, but that's exactly what Jax did. He'd never been on this particular part of Herman Dawson's acreage, but he wasn't far from the ranch. Probably only a couple of miles.

The trick would be to make it there ahead of the gunmen.

"Call Chase again," Jax told Paige. "Let him know what's going on."

She did that while Jax continued to maneuver his way around the winding trail. It wasn't meant for vehicles like his but rather as a way for tractors and utility vehicles to get to remote parts of the property. This one clearly hadn't been used in a while because in places there were bushes and weeds several feet high.

"Chase said there's no sign of the gunmen so far," Paige relayed.

Good. Maybe it'd stay that way. In fact, maybe they weren't headed to the ranch but rather the highway so they could escape and regroup. Jax prayed that was the case, anyway.

The minutes and the miles crawled by while Paige and he kept watch around them. She kept glancing at the phone, too. If it rang, it could be bad news, but thankfully there was no call from Chase by the time Jax reached the road. The second he was on the asphalt again, he gunned the engine.

Jax spotted some armed ranch hands when he made the final turn and drove past his house. The CSI van was parked in the driveway. They had no doubt still been searching for any other cameras or bugs when the gunman had climbed over the fence. Now they'd be processing the scene of a shooting. But Jax couldn't feel bad about a dead gunman. He would have shot the man himself to stop him from getting near his family.

There were ranch hands at the main house, too, and Chase and Levi were waiting for them just inside the door. Thankfully, there were no signs of the gunmen who'd just attacked them.

"Everyone's fine," Chase said right off. "Matthew's having fun with all the attention he's getting."

Good. That was something at least.

As he'd done since this whole mess had started, Jax got Paige inside the house. And that's when he noticed the blood. There was a streak of it running down the side of her head.

Damn.

It'd probably happened when her head hit the dash. But Paige obviously hadn't noticed, and she would have rushed to find Matthew if Jax hadn't stopped her.

"Matthew shouldn't see you like that," he told her.

The words obviously didn't get through to her. Even though Paige was still struggling to get away from him, Jax led her into the nearby powder room, and she froze when she caught a glimpse of herself in the mirror.

"Oh, God." She leaned in, examining it while Jax took a hand towel and wet it.

"I think you might have popped a stitch," he said, dabbing at the wound. "And it looks as if you have a new cut, too. I'll need to get the medic out here."

He reached for his phone, only to realize Paige still had it. And she wasn't just holding it; she had a death grip on it. Her hands were shaking, and she was fighting back tears.

"I'm not going to cry," she insisted. She practically dropped the phone on the vanity. "I don't want Matthew or your family to see me crying."

Jax was sure he didn't want to see it, either, but he was surprised she hadn't broken down by now. "Just take a minute," he said, because he didn't know what else to say. He shut the door to give her a little privacy while she pulled herself together.

Paige gulped in several long breaths, blinked hard against those threatening tears. "I might need a year to steady my nerves."

Yeah. He might need longer. And while he wasn't a fix for raw nerves, Jax eased her into his arms for a hug. She melted right against him, as if she'd never been away from him. That was the trouble with hugs. With being close to her like this. And yet Jax needed it as much as he thought she did.

They stood there, several moments, and when Jax's lungs started to ache, he realized he was holding his breath. He inched back, meeting her gaze. No tears. And the bleeding had stopped. That should have been his cue to move away from her.

He didn't, though.

Jax didn't see the kiss coming. But he sure as hell felt it. The moment Paige put her mouth to his, he hooked his arm around her, dragging her closer. The frustration was there. She didn't want to be doing this. She didn't want to want him.

But she did.

Jax was right there with her. In regard to both the frustration and the want. Except his was more of a need. Always was when it came to Paige.

She was the one who moved back. "Wow," she said, her voice silky soft. "Your kisses always did pack a punch."

But for some reason he didn't think a punch was nearly enough. He hauled her back to him, and he kissed her again. Now, here was the cure for the nightmarish images in his head. The taste of her kicked out all of the bad stuff, and he was suddenly lost in the heat.

Paige made that sound of pleasure. One he knew all too well. Because he'd heard that sound a lot when they were having sex. Of course, just the reminder of it made his body start suggesting that sex might be just what they needed right now.

Of course, his body was wrong.

But that didn't stop him. Didn't stop Paige, either. It was as if they were pouring every bit of their fears and frustrations into that kiss. Her arms tightened around him again, but Jax did his own share of holding her. Keeping her right against him. Body to body.

Yeah.

This was what he wanted.

And even though he knew it was wrong, he deepened the kiss and touched her. His hand sliding over her breasts. His hands wanted to go a whole lot lower than that, though.

That was the problem with Paige being his ex. They knew all the right spots to drive each other crazy. Paige took her mouth to his neck. Jax dropped his hands to her lower back, aligning them just right so that his erection was in the right place, too.

She made that silky sound of pleasure again. The one that made him want to push this even further. Something that couldn't happen.

At least not in a powder room with his family in the house. Besides, there were plenty of other things he needed to be doing, and Paige wasn't exactly in any shape to be making out with him. That didn't stop him, but it slowed him down so he could come to his senses.

Jax gave her one last kiss and moved back.

This was probably a good time for him to admit that the kissing had been a mistake, but he didn't have a chance to say anything because there was a soft knock at the door.

"You two okay?" Chase asked.

That moved them even farther apart. Not that there was a ton of room for them to separate. They were still way too close. Jax gave her a second. Gave himself one, too, before he opened the door.

"We're fine," he said to Chase.

Chase eyed him, then Paige, and grumbled something under his breath that Jax didn't catch. A reminder that his family, or at least Chase, wasn't on board with his getting involved with Paige again. It wouldn't do any good to tell Chase that it was the attraction and not anything that Paige and he had consciously decided to do. But Chase likely already knew that, anyway.

"I called for a medic," Chase explained. "He should be here soon to check those stitches."

Paige looked ready to argue about that, but she must have realized it'd be a lost cause. She was seeing a medic.

"Is the house locked up?" Jax asked.

Chase nodded. "I reset the security system, too. Levi's standing guard by the front door. Weston is at the back."

"And what about Cord?" Paige pressed.

"He left right before you got here. He's dropping off that camera for Jericho before he heads out to look for those gunmen who attacked you."

Jax welcomed any and all help, though he figured those men were long gone since they hadn't shown up by now.

"Come on." Jax put his hand on Paige's back to get her moving. "I'll take you to the playroom so you can see Matthew."

"What about going to a safe house?" Chase asked, following them.

Paige immediately shook her head. "It isn't a good idea for Matthew to be out there right now. There could be more of those thugs waiting to attack, and this time we might not get so lucky."

Jax agreed. Having their son at the ranch house wasn't ideal, but with all their layers of security, Matthew was safer here than he was out on the road. At least until they could track down those gunmen.

When they made it to the playroom, Matthew spotted them the second they stepped into the doorway, and he raced out of his grandmother's arms toward them. "Mommy, Daddy," he said, hurrying to them.

Jax scooped him up and kissed him before he moved him closer to Paige so she could do the same. Matthew's attention went straight to the wound on Paige's head.

"Boo boo," he said, but it didn't hold his attention for long. Matthew reached for Jax's badge, and Jax unclipped it so he could play with it.

Not that he needed any playthings.

The room was filled with all kinds of toys to accommodate his mom's grandchildren. Jericho's son. Chase's daughter. Matthew. And now Addie's son, who was sleeping in the playpen.

Jax handed off Matthew to Paige, and he could practically see some of the tension fade from her face. She kissed Matthew again and joined Alexa and Addie on the sofa. Jax stepped out into the hall with Chase.

"What about Herman Dawson?" Jax asked. "Did the fire department make it to his place?"

Chase nodded. "Herman wasn't there. No one was. The house was totaled, though."

Herman's home was gone, and all because somebody wanted to use the smoke to help set a trap.

"There could be a problem with Belinda," Chase said a moment later, getting Jax's attention. "While Paige and you were…in the bathroom, Jericho called, and he said Belinda left."

"What do you mean she left?" Jax snapped.

"She had a short chat with Jericho and told him her prints might be on the camera that was found under the porch swing. After that, she excused herself, saying she needed to lie down in the break room, and she sneaked out the back."

That got his attention, too, and not in a good way. Jax would address the part about her leaving, but first he wanted to hear about that camera. "Did she have a good reason as to why her prints would be on it?"

"No. But she had a bad one. She said she dropped something while she was on the porch, saw it beneath the swing but thought it was some kind of hardware to hold the swing in place."

"And she touched it?" Jax didn't bother to take the skepticism out of his voice.

"You think she could have really been the one to put that camera in place?" Chase went on.

"Maybe." But for him to believe that, he would also have to accept that she might indeed want Paige dead.

Except there was a problem with that.

Those gunmen had been trying to kill both Paige and him, so that would mean Belinda could want him dead, too. It put a huge knot in his stomach to even consider it. This was the woman he'd trusted with his son. Trusted with nearly every aspect of his life. Could she have betrayed him because she was jealous?

Or was she innocent in all of this?

Even though Paige couldn't hear their conversation, she looked at them, the concern in her eyes again. Probably because she saw the concern on his own face. He'd have to tell her about this, but it could wait for now so she could have some moments with Matthew.

"Belinda could be in grave danger," Jax admitted. "If she was telling the truth about not setting up that camera and the truth about the intruder being in her house, she could have a killer after her. So, would she just sneak out of the sheriff's office?"

Chase shrugged. "Giving her the benefit of the doubt, she could have panicked. Unlike the rest of us, she's never had anyone gunning for her before. Added to that, she might feel a little, well, betrayed by you." He immediately held up his hands in defense. "Hey, I didn't say it was true. I was just looking at this from her perspective."

Yeah. And Jax tried to do that, too. Maybe Belinda sensed the attraction still there between Paige and him. Jax took out his phone and pressed Belinda's number. If she answered, maybe he could talk some sense into her. But she didn't answer. His call went straight to her voice mail.

"Anyway, Dexter's out looking for Belinda," Chase went on. "He can't force her to agree to protective custody, but he'll try to talk her into it."

Maybe he could. Belinda wasn't an idiot. And that reminder didn't help the niggling feeling in his gut. If she truly thought she was in danger, why would she have left the group of people who could protect her?

"Belinda could have lied about having an intruder," Chase tossed out there. "Not because she's behind the plot to kill Paige but because she wanted to get some attention from you. When that failed, she could have decided to cut her losses and get out of there."

Sadly, that was the best-case scenario in all of this. Belinda was innocent, and no one wanted her dead.

"Where's this thing leading with Paige and you, anyway?" Chase asked a moment later.

Normally, he wouldn't have minded his brother prying into his private life, but this wasn't exactly a private thing. Being around Paige put them all in danger. "I'm not sure," Jax confessed. "I kissed her. Twice."

Chase made an *hmmp* sound. "I figured you'd already done more than that."

"Not yet," he mumbled.

And he wished that was a joke. It wasn't. Because while his brain was telling him it'd be a mistake, Jax could feel himself on a collision course. One that would land him in bed with Paige.

His phone buzzed, and Jax expected it to be an update from Jericho. It wasn't. "Unknown caller" was on the screen.

His heart slammed against his chest, and Paige must have noticed his reaction because she left Matthew playing on the floor and hurried over to him. When Jax showed her the screen, she jerked in her breath and held it.

Jax didn't want to answer the call. Didn't want to hear the killer, or rather someone pretending to be the Moonlight Strangler, taunt Paige again. But he didn't have a choice here. Every conversation was a chance to figure out who this person was. And Paige must have realized that, too, because she led Jax away from the playroom door. No doubt so their son wouldn't be able to hear any part of this. She motioned for Jax to hit the answer button, and he put the call on speaker.

"Jax," the caller immediately said. "Don't bother to trace this. I'm using another burner."

Hell. It was the same person who'd talked to Paige earlier at the sheriff's office. The real Moonlight Strangler.

"Paige, are you there?" he asked. "Of course you are. You're not leaving Jax's side. Well, unless I can entice you with an offer."

"What do you want?" she asked. Not much emotion in her voice, but it was all over her face, and every muscle in her body had gone stiff.

"You want these attacks on Jax and you to stop? Do you want to know who's behind them? Then meet with me."

Jax wanted to curse. Of course this monster would want that.

"You want to meet with me so you can kill me," Paige said. Not a question.

"Now, now." Unlike Paige's, there was emotion in the killer's voice. Sugary sweet and sickening. "I said I wasn't ready to do that yet, and I'm not. Have I ever lied to you before?"

"No," she admitted after several moments.

"But that doesn't mean she'll trust you," Jax snapped. "If you really know who's trying to kill us, just tell us. I'm sure you want us to stop the person pretending to be you."

"Oh, then I'd miss the chance to see Paige up close and personal again, wouldn't I?" he taunted.

Jax couldn't hold back the profanity. Profanity that caused this snake to laugh. This was all a game to him.

"Now, about that meeting," the killer went on. "Here's your chance to end the danger, to keep your little boy safe. Meet me at the location I'm about to text you. Oh, and you can bring Jax. One of his brothers, too, if you like, but I'd advise against trying to set a trap. Because, you see, I'll have a hostage. One I hadn't planned on killing, but I will if you don't show up."

"Who did you take?" Jax snapped.

Hell. Had he taken Belinda? Or maybe the Moonlight Strangler had managed to get to someone in his family. Jax motioned for Chase to start checking, and his brother stepped away, already taking out his phone.

"The hostage will be in touch with you, too," the

killer added. "I'm thinking a call like that might convince you to come. Look for that text, Paige." He ended the call, leaving Paige and Jax standing there, staring at the phone.

"You're not meeting with him," Jax said just in case Paige had some stupid notion about doing that.

And apparently, she did. "You heard him. He has a hostage."

"He's a killer," Jax fired back, but the words had no sooner left his mouth when his phone dinged, indicating he had a text message.

"'Meet me by your grave, Paige,'" Jax read aloud. "'I'm giving you one hour, but I wouldn't wait too long. The hostage seems to be having trouble breathing. As I said, bring Jax, his brother. Hell, bring anybody you want. Just show up, let me see your pretty face and I'll give you both the hostage and the information.'"

Jax had to curse again. This SOB really wanted to twist the knife into Paige. Maybe literally.

"My grave is in the cemetery at the church near here?" she asked.

He nodded. It was where other family members had been buried, and even though Paige had been his ex-wife, Jax had figured that one day he would want to show Matthew her headstone.

"But the old church isn't there any longer," Jax explained. "Long story but someone blew it up a couple of months back. They're rebuilding it, but it's just a construction site right now."

Which, of course, meant there were plenty of places for a killer to lie in wait.

Jax got right in Paige's face so she could see that he wasn't going to let this meeting happen. "You know what he's trying to do. He wants you dead."

She lifted her shoulder. "He was right about never having lied to me. And we both know he hates people using him to take the blame for these attacks. He might be planning on turning the person over to us."

"And he might just gun you down the second you get there!" he huffed, ready to gear up for more of that, but the phone rang.

Not his cell but Chase's. Since it could be one of the ranch hands calling about another intruder, Jax went to him. And judging from his brother's concerned expression, something had indeed gone wrong.

"It's Cord," Chase said, holding out his phone while he pressed the speaker function.

"Don't come here to save me," Cord immediately said. He didn't sound right. Not his usual iceman self. He grunted and gulped in his breath. Cord was in pain. "No matter what he says to you or does to me, don't come."

"Where are you?" Paige asked, though Jax was certain she already knew the answer.

It took Cord several seconds to respond, and there were more of those sounds that Jax didn't want to hear. "At the church. I'm the hostage."

Chapter Thirteen

"I have to do this," Paige said, something she'd been repeating to Jax for the past thirty minutes. "And we don't have much time. Cord could be dying."

She knew that wasn't an argument Jax wanted to hear. He wasn't fond of Cord, but Jax was a lawman and he wouldn't want the Moonlight Strangler to claim another victim.

Including Cord.

God, she hated to think of what that monster had done to him. And all because of her. Cord had been good to her, he'd tried to help her and now he could be dying.

"Jericho and Dexter just arrived at the road near the church," Chase told them when he finished his latest call. At least Chase was cooperating with her plans to go to the meeting and had scrambled to start getting security in place, not just at the church but here at the ranch, too.

"She's not changing her mind about this," Chase added to Jax. "Would you stay put if you knew you could save a man's life?"

"I would if it meant saving hers," Jax fired back. He cursed right after that outburst, something he'd been doing a lot in the past couple of minutes.

Chase stepped away from them. Maybe to give her time to win Jax over to what could turn out to be a deadly plan. Or maybe Chase was just tired of hearing them argue, especially since he'd already told them that he'd be going to this meeting with her.

"I don't want you to do this." Jax slipped his hand around the back of her neck, holding her in place to make eye contact with her.

"I don't want to do it, either, but I don't have a choice. I couldn't live with myself if he murdered Cord, or anyone else, just because I didn't have the guts to show up and face him. And you wouldn't be able to live with yourself, either."

She stepped away from him to let that sink in, and Paige went into the playroom to kiss Matthew—twice. He had fallen asleep on the sofa, obviously worn-out from his play session.

"We'll take good care of him," Addie offered. "Just be careful." And she kissed Paige on the cheek.

Somehow, Paige managed to thank her despite the lump in her throat, and when she went back into the hall, Chase and Jax were there. Chase handed her a Kevlar vest. Both Chase and Jax already had one on.

"You're wearing it," Jax snarled, the muscles in his jaw at war with each other. He took her hand and put a gun in it. "And you'll be behind me the whole time.

If anything, and I mean anything, goes wrong, you'll get down and stay down."

She wasn't sure if her last argument had won him over or if it was something Chase had said. Either way, this meeting was going to happen. And Paige prayed they all survived it.

"Move fast," Jax told her, and the three of them got moving out the door. Not to the cruiser. It was too shot up. But rather into one of the family's SUVs.

Levi locked up the house as soon as they were out, and he no doubt set the security system. She counted eight ranch hands outside the house. All armed. All looking ready in case there was another attack. With Levi and Weston inside the house, maybe that would be enough to keep everyone safe.

"Jericho let the hospital know that Cord might need an ambulance," Chase explained once Jax got them moving away from the house. "But obviously the paramedics can't just go driving in there."

No. Because they might be shot. Still, maybe they'd be close by and able to respond if all of this came to a quick end.

"Maybe Cord isn't hurt as bad as he sounded," she said, thinking out loud now. "He carries a backup weapon in his boot, and maybe he still has it. Maybe he'll get a chance to use it."

"Too many *maybes*," Jax commented under his breath. "And Cord didn't want you to do this. No lawman would."

But thankfully Jax kept driving, the SUV eating up

the distance between the ranch and the church. Which wasn't much distance at all. Just a couple of miles. However, it was more than enough time for the flashbacks to come.

God.

Would they never go away?

Would there ever be a time when she didn't feel this paralyzing fear? It was yet another *maybe*, but perhaps if she faced down this monster, the flashbacks would stop. Of course, he might just give her a new set of memories. A new reason to have flashbacks.

First, though, she had to survive. Cord, too. And somehow she had to keep Jax and Chase out of harm's way.

Jax turned off the road, and she immediately spotted the cruiser, and Jax pulled up along beside it. Jericho was behind the wheel, and Dexter was in the passenger's seat. Both were wearing Kevlar, too.

"Any sign of them?" Jax asked his brother.

Jericho shook his head. "Not yet. But I figure the Moonlight Strangler was in place before he even called you."

Paige figured the same thing. Whatever he'd set up—either a meeting or a trap—the killer had everything just as he wanted it.

"Two Texas Rangers are on the way," Jericho explained. "And an FBI agent out of the San Antonio office. They should be here soon, and I told them to do a silent approach."

Six lawmen. Paige hoped that would be enough to put an end to this once and for all.

But certainly the Moonlight Strangler had known this would happen. Every law enforcement agency in the country was looking for him, and he'd invited her to bring them along.

That didn't help with the acid churning in her stomach.

What was this sick fool planning?

"Follow me," Jax told his brother. "Keep watch behind us."

Jericho nodded, and they all got moving again. It was only about a hundred yards before Jax rounded a curve and she saw the church. Or rather where the church had once stood. Paige was very familiar with it since it was where she and Jax had gotten married. But it was now indeed a construction site.

She didn't see any workers. In fact, she didn't see anyone at all, but there were three huge piles of building materials, all covered with black tarp. The killer could be hiding beneath any one of those.

Or in the cemetery.

Jax pulled to a stop about fifty yards away. But he didn't turn off the engine. They just sat there and waited.

They didn't have to wait long.

Jax's phone buzzed, and she saw "Unknown caller" on the screen. Jax answered it without taking his attention off their surroundings.

"Paige," the killer said, his voice oozing from the

other end of the line. It was the Moonlight Strangler all right. "You came."

She cleared her throat before she even attempted to answer. "Of course I came. You didn't give me much of a choice. Now, where's Cord? And where are you?"

The silence dragged on for so long that Paige thought for a moment that he'd hung up. But he hadn't.

"I'm here," he answered.

There was some movement. Not near the church or cemetery, but way back. Hundreds of yards away in a cluster of trees.

It was cloudy, there was a storm moving in, and what thread of sunlight there was didn't help much. All she could see was a silhouette. But it was a man all right, and he was holding a phone to his ear. Even though she hadn't gotten a good look at the man who left her for dead, she'd gotten a sense of his height and weight.

"Oh, God," Paige whispered. She couldn't stop herself from gasping. "It's him. It's really the Moonlight Strangler."

"Of course it's really me, sweetheart," the man said.

And it was. Jax had no doubts about it when he heard the man speak. It was the same voice from the earlier calls.

Jax took out binoculars from the glove compartment for a closer look. The guy was about six feet tall, medium build and had brown hair. He was wearing jeans and a gray shirt. The description that came to mind was average-looking.

But this guy was far from average.

Nor did he stay in their line of sight for long. He ducked back behind one of the trees.

Paige swallowed hard, but Jax had to give it to her. She wasn't panicking, and she hiked up her chin, trying to look a whole lot stronger than she probably felt at the moment.

"You're not at my grave where you told me to meet you," Paige reminded the man.

"No. I thought it best if I stayed back at bit. Those cowboys do like to shoot people, don't they?"

"They do," Jax assured him. And that's exactly what he would do if he got the chance. But the snake was out of range, and that's almost certainly why he'd taken up position there.

That, and he might have some backup in the woods behind him. In the past, the Moonlight Strangler had acted alone—or at least there'd never been any evidence of him teaming up with anyone—but this wasn't just an ordinary situation for him. He wanted to get another shot at killing Paige.

"All right, here's how this will work," the killer continued. "Paige, I want you to step out of the SUV. You can hide behind any lawman of your choosing. Just one, though. I want to see your face, and I can't do that if there's a wall of badges in front of you."

"Release Cord first," she spoke up before Jax could say anything. "I want to make sure he's alive."

"Oh, he's alive all right. Maybe not all in one piece, exactly. But he will live if you do what I tell you and don't dawdle. He's bleeding out."

Her breath caught, and her bottom lip trembled. "I still want to see him before I get out."

Her gaze connected with Jax's for just a second, and he knew what she was aiming for here. She didn't just want to see Cord, though that was critical. She wanted to try to get Cord to safety so he'd be out of the line of fire.

The moments crawled by with no word from the killer. Then Jax saw the movement in the same area where the Moonlight Strangler had disappeared.

Cord.

Using the binoculars again, Jax could see the blood. On Cord's face. On the front of his clothes. Cord glanced up at them and shook his head.

Damn.

Was that some kind of signal?

Jax didn't have time to find out. Cord stumbled, falling about five yards in front of where the Moonlight Strangler had been earlier.

"Don't worry," the killer said. "He's alive. For now."

Maybe so, but he also appeared to have been drugged. He tried to get up but collapsed.

"What did you do to him?" Paige snapped.

"Oh, he's not hurt that bad. But I did have to medicate him a little so he wouldn't try to escape. Or kill. The boy's a real fighter. The meds will wear off in an hour or two."

They didn't have that long. The killer hadn't lied about Cord's condition. He appeared to be bleeding out.

"Now it's your turn, Paige. Step out, let me see you and I'll tell you the name of the real person who's been trying to murder you."

Paige stared at Cord, no doubt praying that he would move farther away from his captor. Jax adjusted the binoculars and spotted the reason Cord wasn't trying to do just that.

"There's a rope tied around his leg," Jax explained. "And the other end of the rope is around a tree. That's as far as Cord can go."

"Time's a-wasting, Paige," the killer snarled. Not so much of a taunt now. His temper was coming through.

Jax was about to remind her of the dangers again and that this might all be for nothing. The Moonlight Strangler could gun Cord down at any time. Plus, this piece of dirt might not even know who was behind the attacks.

But Jax stayed quiet. There was nothing he could say that would talk her out of this. Paige might have a boatload of emotional baggage, but she wasn't a coward. Never had been. In hindsight, it was one of the reasons he'd first been attracted to her.

And this was a hell of a time for him to realize that.

"I'll be in front of you," Jax insisted. He would take the killer up on that particular offer.

She didn't argue. Probably because she knew it was the only way he'd let her out there. "If something goes wrong—"

"Don't," he interrupted. It sounded like the start of a goodbye. Something he didn't want to hear.

Jax put the SUV in gear, maneuvering it so that the driver's side was facing the killer. Or at least facing where the killer had been earlier. It was possible the guy had moved.

And Jax opened the door.

Though he was still out of range, he already had his gun drawn, and he slipped his phone into his pocket to free his hands and stepped from the SUV.

No shots.

That was a surprise and somewhat of a relief. Jax had half expected this moron to start shooting. Or maybe he was just waiting for Paige before he pulled the trigger.

Paige's grip on her gun had caused her knuckles to go white. She was still shaking, too. That didn't stop her from getting out behind him. Thankfully, she didn't move to Jax's side. She stayed behind him.

"Can't see your face," the killer complained, though his voice was muffled now because Jax's phone was in his pocket. "At least stand on your tippy-toes so I can get a good look at you. I wouldn't put it past your ex to try to bring in a ringer."

"It's me," she assured him. "And you'll see me when I see you."

Jax mentally groaned. Yeah, courage all right. But this was one time when he wished she'd just shown her face and ducked back in the SUV. Maybe she was hoping Jericho, Chase or Dexter would have a shot.

They didn't.

And even if they did, Jax was betting this coward would just slink behind one of those trees and escape. Because there's no way the Moonlight Strangler would have come out here without an escape plan.

"Awww, you want to see me?" the killer purred. "How sweet. All right. Just one little look-see, though I'm not sure how much you can see without those binoculars."

"I'll see enough," she snapped.

Even though Jax kept his attention and gun aimed at those trees, he felt Paige move, coming up on tiptoes so that the killer could see her.

"There she is," the killer said. No more temper. It was the tone one might use with an old lover. "And my mark looks so good on you. One day we'll meet again, and I'll get to finish it."

Her muscles tensed even more. "Now it's your turn. I've done everything you asked. Tell me who's behind the attacks so we can get Cord to the hospital."

Jax wasn't sure he saw the man move. Or maybe he just sensed it. But it seemed to take only the blink of an eye for the killer to whip out a rifle.

Hell.

He was going to shoot her.

Jax moved as fast as he could to push Paige back into the SUV. But the killer and he weren't the only ones moving. From the corner of his eye, he saw Cord.

Cord reached for his boot. He no longer seemed

drugged. He pulled out his backup weapon, turned and fired. And he just kept firing.

Each of the bullets slamming into the killer.

The Moonlight Strangler clutched his chest and collapsed onto the ground.

Chapter Fourteen

Paige couldn't stop shaking. Or pacing in the ER waiting room. Her heartbeat was going a mile a minute. Her thoughts, too. Especially the bad thoughts.

Cord might be dead, or dying.

So she paced and waited for news. Oh, and she prayed, as well. She'd been doing a lot of that in the past half hour since they'd arrived at the Appaloosa Pass Hospital.

The medic had already suggested to Jax that she might be going into shock and that she should be checked out by a doctor. But Paige didn't want a checkup. She didn't want to stop moving in case she fell completely apart. As long as she was on her feet and moving, she could expend some of that raw adrenaline and energy boiling inside her.

Jax finished his latest call and went to her, slipping his arm around her and trying to get her into one of the many empty chairs. But she didn't budge, and as he'd done on his other attempts, Jax pulled her to him for a hug.

That helped.

But knowing that Cord was all right would help even more.

The ambulance had been there within minutes after the shooting, and they'd whisked Cord away to the hospital. Jax and she had left to follow it, but she hadn't even managed to get a glimpse of Cord before he'd been taken into surgery for the multiple stab wounds to his chest.

Jax pulled her even closer, and she felt the tension in his muscles then. Of course, they were both tense, but this was different. She pulled back, met his gaze and saw the worry, or something, in his eyes.

"What's wrong?" Oh, God. "Is it Matthew—"

"He's fine. Everyone at the ranch is fine, and Addie is on her way here to see Cord."

Addie would want to be here, of course. Cord was her biological twin brother.

"It's the Moonlight Strangler," Jax continued a moment later. He paused, for a long time. "He's alive."

Of all the things she thought he might say, that wasn't one of them. "How? We saw him fall."

Jax nodded. "I just got off the phone with Jericho, and he said when he checked, the killer had a pulse, so he called another ambulance. They're bringing him here to the hospital right now."

Her heart skipped several beats, and she had no choice but to fall back into Jax's arms. He was there to catch her.

"You won't see him. The paramedics have been in-structed to bring him in through a side entrance."

Paige was shaking her head before he even finished, and not because she was worried about seeing him. "He's dangerous. He could kill someone here."

Jax was shaking his head, too. "He's not even con-scious. And he might not survive the ambulance ride. Jericho said he lost a lot of blood."

She wanted him dead, not clinging to life.

Paige groaned and finally sat down, only because her legs were wobbly and she was dizzy. But then she considered something else.

"Maybe he can tell us who orchestrated the attacks." Yes, it was wishful thinking, and she wasn't sure she wanted him to draw another breath, much less to have to speak to him again. Still, if he could just tell them.

"He could have been lying about what he knew any-way," Jax reminded her. "He clearly set all of this up to kill you. That's why he had that rifle."

Yes, that. She'd gotten a glimpse of it. Of Cord, too, as he'd shot the man. His own father. But Cord didn't think of him that way, only that he was a mon-ster who needed to be stopped. He'd devoted the last year of his life to catching him, and in a roundabout way, he'd succeeded.

Paige couldn't help but think of the similarities between Cord and her. She'd been obsessed with the Moonlight Strangler, too. And she'd found him. Of course, he'd found her as well and had come within a breath of making her number thirty-one.

Well, at least now there wouldn't be more bodies to add to his count.

"He had a wallet in his pocket," Jax went on. "According to his driver's license, his name is Willie Lee Samuels. Does that sound familiar?"

It was stupid, but she didn't even want to repeat it. Didn't want to have his name come out of her mouth. But Paige forced herself to think, to dig through her memories and see if there was a connection. Was it familiar?

No.

"I don't know that name, and I didn't recognize his face, either. Only his voice and the overall size of his body. I could be mistaken about the body size, of course, but that was his voice, Jax. I swear, it was him."

Paige hadn't realized she was starting to sound a little hysterical until Jax sat down beside her and pulled her back into his arms.

"His face matches his DMV photo," Jax went on. "But his DNA will be sent for testing even though they're almost positive he's the Moonlight Strangler."

So was she. No way could Paige forget that voice. It would almost certainly be added to the flashbacks of the previous attacks. Along with that blood on Cord's face and chest.

"Jericho checked, and he doesn't have a police record. Not even a parking ticket," Jax added.

Ironic. Since he'd murdered so many women. And would have murdered her if Cord hadn't stopped him.

Paige heard the hurried footsteps, and she automatically tensed. So did Jax, and he put his hand over his Glock. But it was a false alarm. Addie came rushing into the ER.

"How's Cord?" Addie asked, her breath mixed with her words.

"He's in surgery." Paige stood and pulled Addie into her arms. "We'll know something soon." She hoped.

"How bad was he hurt?" Addie pressed. A sister's love, and worry, were all over her face.

"He was bleeding," Paige settled for saying, "but he was strong enough to shoot the Moonlight Strangler. He saved us. He saved all of us."

And despite the fact that tears were the last thing she needed, they watered her eyes, anyway. Addie's, too.

"Addie insisted on coming," Levi said. He trailed in right behind her, and just his mere presence gave Paige another jolt.

"Who's at the ranch with Matthew?" Paige snapped.

"Weston and a whole bunch of ranch hands armed with rifles and automatics. The two reserve deputies should be there by now, too."

Good. She knew that the sheriff's office had to be stretched for manpower, but she didn't care. Paige wanted Matthew and the rest of Jax's family to be safe.

Addie pulled back from the hug and met Paige's gaze. "Did you see *him*?" Addie asked.

It took Paige a moment to realize Addie was talking about the killer and not Cord. Paige nodded. "From a distance."

She wasn't sure what Addie wanted to know about

the monster who'd fathered her. Maybe nothing that could be said in words, anyway, because Addie just held on to her, and they stayed that way until Paige heard yet more footsteps.

This time both Levi and Jax put their hands over their guns. And it wasn't family who came rushing in.

It was Leland.

His face was beaded with sweat, and his attention zoomed around the room until it landed on her. "Thank God. You're all right. I heard about the attack."

Leland moved toward her, but Jax stepped in front of him, blocking his path.

"Hell." Leland mumbled even more profanity, too. "You can't still think I want to hurt Paige. It was the Moonlight Strangler all along. Can't you see that?"

Paige wanted to *see* it. To believe it. But the attack was still way too fresh in her mind for her to trust anyone except family.

But she immediately rethought that.

Jax's family. They weren't her in-laws any longer, but this had certainly brought them closer. Well, at least they weren't scowling at her, and maybe they were beginning to understand that she'd stayed away to protect them.

Maybe.

Leland continued to stare at her. Mixing in a glare, too. Likely waiting for her to say he was innocent. She didn't, but Paige did go closer to him.

"You shouldn't be here," she said.

The glare vanished, but she saw the hurt again. The

same hurt look he'd gotten a few days earlier when she told him that she could never have feelings beyond friendship for him. The rejection still stung.

He glanced around as if trying to compose himself, and then hitched his thumb toward the parking lot. "There are reporters outside. Darrin was out there, too, but I told him if he tried to come in that I'd arrest him."

Both Jax and she groaned. She definitely didn't need a run-in with Darrin right now, and she doubted Jericho would be able to interrogate him anytime soon. Not after the hellish ordeal they'd all just been through.

"Do you need anything?" Leland asked. "Tea?" He glanced at her top. "A change of clothes?"

She hadn't realized there was blood on her shirt. Cord's blood. She'd hurried to him after he'd shot the Moonlight Strangler and had tried to help him before the ambulance arrived. Jax had done the same, and there was blood on his shirt, too, on the places that their Kevlar vests hadn't covered. The vests had blood on them as well, but they'd left them in the SUV.

"If Paige needs anything," Jax said, staring at the man, "I'll get it for her."

This wasn't a jealousy, man-contest kind of thing going on between them. Jax was just worried about her safety. But Leland clearly didn't like it. No surprise there. He hadn't liked much of anything Jax had said to him. For Leland, it was indeed jealousy.

Leland started to step away, but Jax stopped him. "Any idea where Belinda went after she sneaked out of the sheriff's office?"

"None," Leland snapped. "Are you accusing me of trying to hurt her?"

"Just asking." But it certainly wasn't a friendly sounding question.

"If you're worried about her, find her yourself," Leland snarled before he walked out.

"You want me to follow him and make sure he leaves?" Levi asked.

Jax seemed to be still considering that when Jericho came in. Not from the ER entrance but rather from one of the halls that fed off the waiting area. He, too, had some blood on his shirt, and he was carrying an evidence bag.

"Willie Lee Samuels is in a coma," Jericho immediately volunteered.

In a coma. But not dead. For Paige, that wasn't good news. "He could be faking it," she suggested.

"I thought so, too, but the doc who just checked him said it was the real deal. So are the three bullets that Cord put in his chest. Don't worry. I'll have a guard posted outside surgery just in case, and the FBI is sending a protection detail from the San Antonio office. They should be here within the half hour."

Good. She prayed they didn't let the Moonlight Strangler out of their sight.

Jericho lifted the evidence bag, and since it was clear plastic, Paige saw the one item inside it. A driver's license.

"Yeah, it belongs to Willie Lee Samuels," Jericho confirmed. "Either of you recognize him from the photo?"

Addie took the bag as if it might explode in her hands. Paige looked as well, and while she didn't recognize the man, she did see something familiar about him. Addie must have, as well.

"He looks like Cord and me. We have his eyes." Addie's hand was shaking when she handed the bag back to Jericho. "I'd hoped…"

But she didn't finish that. No need. Because Paige knew what she'd hoped—that she didn't share any DNA with this sick man. That it had all been a big mistake.

Willie Lee Samuels's face proved otherwise.

"So, it's really over," Addie whispered. She blew out a long breath of relief.

But it was relief that Jericho didn't share. His forehead was bunched up, and he took out a notepad from his pocket. "Dexter took Willie Lee's phone to the office so the lab could pick it up for processing, but I looked through the numbers he'd called. Just two. There was the call he made to Paige, and then he called this number."

As he'd done with the driver's license, Jericho held it up for them to see.

Both Addie and Paige shook their heads, but Jax didn't. He took one look at the number and cursed.

Chapter Fifteen

Belinda.

Jax had no idea why the Moonlight Strangler had called her earlier in the day, and he was no closer to finding that out. Because Belinda was nowhere to be found. Since it was already dark and a storm had moved in, there wouldn't be much more searching done for her tonight.

There wouldn't be much sleep for Paige, either.

With all the pacing she'd done at the hospital, Jax was surprised that her legs hadn't given out on her. Surprised, too, that she hadn't just broken down and cried. The adrenaline crash had come and gone—for him, too—leaving them both looking past the exhausted stage.

"Cord will be all right," he reminded her, hoping that would help get that weary look off her face.

And it was true. Despite his blood loss, he'd come out of surgery just fine, and there'd been no major damage to any of his organs. Of course, Paige knew that. She'd been there for the surgeon's update and even to see Cord when he'd been allowed visitors.

That was the good news.

The bad news was that the Moonlight Strangler was still alive and in a coma.

Paige looked at Jax. Only for a second. Before her attention went back to the road. Or rather their surroundings. Something that both of them had been doing since they'd started the drive from the hospital back to the ranch.

They were in a cruiser now, not the SUV they'd used to go to the hospital. But what they were missing was backup. There just hadn't been anyone available what with the investigation and the security at both the hospital and the ranch. Plus, Jericho had the courier still in lockup and was having to deal with that. And the search for Belinda. While trying to keep an eye on both Leland and Darrin.

Definitely a full plate.

Neither Jax nor Paige had wanted to wait any longer to go home now that Cord was out of the woods. Still, the memories of the other attacks were very fresh, and Jax knew he wouldn't be able to let down his guard until he had Paige safe.

"He's a coward," Paige said.

It took him a moment to realize she was likely talking about the Moonlight Strangler. And yep, Jax agreed. The snake had broken into Cord's vehicle and had ambushed Cord with a stun gun. Then, he'd drugged and stabbed him while Cord hadn't been able to fight back. Of course, Jax hadn't expected a vicious serial killer like that to do anything aboveboard.

Jax took the final turn toward the ranch, checking each side of the road. The ditches, too. Hard to see, though, with the wipers slashing away the rain. Maybe the weather alone would deter another attack. He could hope so, anyway.

And maybe the attacks were over.

It was possible that the Moonlight Strangler had been behind them all along.

"I don't want Matthew to see me like this." Paige motioned to the blood on her clothes and then his.

It was 8:00 p.m., and while it was possible Matthew was already asleep, he might indeed be up and see them. Jax considered calling ahead, but then he spotted the familiar blue truck parked in front of his house. It belonged to his ranch hand Buddy, so Jax pulled up alongside the truck and lowered the passenger's-side window just enough for him to see that Buddy was inside, and armed.

"Jericho asked me to make sure no one got onto the ranch who wasn't supposed to be here," Buddy explained after he put down his window, as well. He pointed to another truck parked just up the road. "Hank's up there."

Hank was a hand, too, one Jax trusted. Jax hated that the men had to do this, but unfortunately it might be necessary.

"Paige and I need to get a change of clothes," Jax said. "Then we'll be heading to the main house for the night."

Buddy nodded. "There are hands guarding up there, too, and we'll stay put until we hear otherwise." He paused. "Some reporters drove up earlier. They had one of those vans with the TV logo on the side and a little satellite dish on top of it. I stopped them, told them to turn around, that it wasn't a good time for a visit."

It was the right thing to do. Nobody in his family was in the mood to deal with reporters right now, though he figured the news frenzy would continue for a while. Especially since the media would be looking to score an interview with Addie, the serial killer's daughter. However, Addie was still at the hospital with Cord, Levi, a reserve deputy and the protection detail from the FBI assigned to guard the Moonlight Strangler.

Jax thanked Buddy, made a mental note to thank all the hands and give them big bonus checks and pulled into the back, parking on the side of the porch next to the porch swing where they'd found that camera and listening device. There was no need to tell Paige to move fast. She knew the drill all too well since running and hiding were all they'd been doing since she'd returned to the ranch.

Jax didn't bother with an umbrella since they'd be changing their clothes, anyway. He got out ahead of her, unlocked the door and disarmed the security system only long enough to get Paige inside. Even though they weren't going to be there long, he reset it and locked the door, too, behind him.

He didn't turn on the lights, just in case someone was indeed watching the house, but he could see that the place was a mess. The CSIs had apparently left no stone unturned when they'd searched for cameras and bugs. Thankfully, other than the one on the porch, they hadn't found anything.

"I'll have to get you one of my shirts," he told her. There were probably some of Belinda's things around, but he doubted she'd want to wear those.

Jax stripped off his shirt and tossed it into the laundry room just off the kitchen. Only then did he realize being shirtless probably wasn't a good idea with Paige in the room.

Or maybe it was.

She looked at him. Looked at his bare chest. And everything inside her finally seemed to go still. She definitely didn't seem ready to start pacing again.

The rain was coming down harder now, slapping against the window. The lightning streaked through the sky, the flashes enough for him to get glimpses of Paige even without the overhead lights.

"I'm a mess," she whispered. Maybe she was talking about her bloody clothes, but it could be a whole lot more.

She turned, the streaks of rain and lighting hitting just right so that it looked as if tears were sliding down her face. Maybe they were. If anyone deserved a good cry, it was her.

But he didn't want her to cry.

He wanted to do something about that stark look on her face. Wanted to do something about her uneven breathing, too. And the nerves. So close to the surface that he could feel them.

He took off his waist holster, laying it on the counter, and went to her. And he kissed her before he could change his mind. All in all, it was a good decision. Paige didn't back away, and she slipped right into his arms. Right into the kiss, as well.

The soft sound she made was one of pleasure. Mostly. Mixed with some doubts that he had no trouble hearing, either. But Jax didn't want doubts. They'd have enough of those later. For now, he just wanted her.

He knew the fix for that. Jax deepened the kiss, bringing her closer to him, and he put his hand at the base of her throat and slid his palm down to her breasts.

Oh, yeah. Familiar territory. But the doubts were still there.

On her part, not his.

"I don't want you to see me naked," she whispered. Her breath shivered. She did, too. "The Moonlight Strangler cut me, and I have scars."

Not an easy thing to hear, but Jax was determined to take some of those old nightmares and put a new light on them. Or at least he'd try. Even if this was probably a bad idea.

He kept kissing her. Kept touching her, too. But Paige did her own share of touching, and like all the other times they'd been together, it didn't take long for the fire to ignite.

Just how long was he going to let that fire burn?

Apparently, pretty damn long, he decided, when her hand landed on his bare chest. Then his stomach.

He turned her, pressing her against the edge of the counter so he could rid her of that bloody top. Jax didn't want any more reminders of the day. What he wanted was her bare skin against his. He took off her bra and lowered the kisses to her breasts.

One of the scars was there. On her left breast. There was another just below it on her rib cage. He kissed both, lingering long enough to make sure she felt only pleasure and not the old memories.

That upped the urgency in him. Upped those silky sounds she was making, too, and she latched on to him and let him add some fuel to the fire. He kissed her stomach, all the while unzipping her jeans, sliding them off her along with her shoes and panties.

Then he kissed her exactly where he wanted.

Her breath broke, and Paige fisted her hand in his hair, and she gave in to the heat for several moments before it must have become too much for her. She dropped down, pulling him to the floor with her, and in the same motion, she went after the zipper on his jeans.

Jax figured he should ask her if she was ready for this, but judging from her nonverbal cues, that answer was yes. She kissed him, shoved off his jeans and boxers, and then straddled him. He could have sworn his head exploded when she took him inside her.

Oh, yeah. He remembered this. Remembered just how good it could be. Of course, sex had never been an issue for them. Apparently, it still wasn't.

She moved, shoving her body against his. Creating the rhythm and the friction needed to make that fire rage out of control. She looked like a woman on a mission.

Maybe she was using this to take out some of her frustrations or to burn off some of that restless energy. Or maybe this was just about them.

Either way, it worked.

She made another sound. Not one of pleasure this time. But release. Jax felt the climax ripple through her. And thanks to a bolt of lightning, he got to see it on her face, as well.

The moment was perfect despite all the imperfections.

And Jax pulled her to him and let himself go with her.

PAIGE COULDN'T MOVE. But she could certainly feel, and that feeling went up a notch when Jax lifted his hips and she got a nice little aftershock from the climax.

Wow.

She hadn't seen this coming, but she didn't have to think long and hard to know it was needed. Jax wasn't just the cure for her headache and tight muscles; he was the cure for other things, too. For the first time in over a year, her mind settled down just enough for her to see and feel something other than the nightmare she'd been living.

Later, she'd decide if that was a good thing.

For now, Paige just savored the moment of her body still joined with Jax's. The feel of his body beneath hers. His scent. That scent alone could stir all sorts of hot thoughts, but it calmed her, too.

Or maybe just the great sex had done that.

However, it didn't last. Jax eased her off him and got up to get his gun and phone. For a second she thought he might just walk away, but he scooped her up, too, and with both of them buck naked, he carried her to the master bathroom. Yet another place she knew well, because she'd come up with the remodel design.

Including the massive stone and tile shower.

Which was exactly where he took her.

Other than a night-light by the vanity, the room was dark, and he kept it that way as he put aside his gun and phone so he could turn on the water. The moment it was hot and steamy, he took her inside, setting her on her feet. Slowly. While her body slid down his.

"Foreplay," he said a split second before he kissed her mouth. Then her neck. "We sort of skipped that in the kitchen."

They'd skipped a lot of things. Like finesse and conversation. But that was okay even if Paige knew that later they were going to have to talk about all of this.

But not now.

For now, she just let him kiss away all the worries. All the pain. And even all the doubts.

Despite the fact that she'd just had him, Paige felt the heat return. Slow and easy like those kisses he was delivering. But he stopped, looking down at her forehead and frowning.

"I don't think you're supposed to be getting those stitches wet," Jax said.

Paige was sure she frowned, too, because it was true, and it caused him to turn off the shower.

"We should be getting dressed, anyway," he added.

Now the doubts came. Not only hers but his. She could practically feel them. But he was also right. They shouldn't be standing around naked even if that was exactly what she wanted to do. Except the sooner they dressed and left, the sooner she'd get to see Matthew.

Jax handed her a towel when they got out of the shower, and after grabbing a towel for himself, he went into the bedroom. Several minutes later he returned, fully dressed in jeans and a black T-shirt. And he handed her not only the clothes she'd taken off in the kitchen, but one of his clean shirts, as well.

Since it felt awkward for her to be standing around naked when he was dressed, Paige hurried to put on the clothes, but she didn't even manage to get her jeans on before Jax's phone buzzed. Considering all the bad news they'd gotten, she immediately thought the worst.

And it likely was.

Because Jax frowned when he glanced at the screen.

"Darrin," he said, showing her the caller ID.

Great. She definitely didn't want to chat with him tonight. Jax must have felt the same way because he let it go to voice mail. Then he listened to the message that Darrin left. He didn't put it on speaker, but judging from the way his teeth came together, it wasn't well wishes.

"Do I want to hear the message for myself?" she asked.

"No," he said without hesitation. "But it wasn't one

of his usual threats. He sounded, well, desperate. He said he needed to see you right away. You're not meeting with him."

"No," she agreed. "Did he say why he wanted to meet?"

Jax shook his head. "But I'm betting it wouldn't be to have a nice conversation. He probably wants you to get Jericho to back off on that interrogation that's scheduled for tomorrow."

An interrogation that might not happen since Jericho was up to his eyeballs with all the stuff going on.

"Sometime soon I should start the process to get a restraining order on Darrin." She paused. Met his gaze. "Or maybe I should wait to see if we'll be moving to that safe house?"

Or better yet, staying in Appaloosa Pass.

Near Matthew and Jax.

Jax didn't answer her. Probably because he heard a sound that caught his attention. Paige heard it, too.

A car engine.

She hoped that it was just Buddy or one of the other hands, but when Jax's phone buzzed and Paige saw Buddy's name on the screen, she figured they had a visitor.

"Put it on speaker so I can hear," she insisted. She wanted to know if they were about to come under attack.

"Anything wrong?" Jax asked when he answered, and he hurried to the living room where there were windows facing the road.

Paige went, too, though Jax motioned for her to stay

back. She did, but she still saw the headlights of the vehicle making its way toward them.

"It's another one of those reporter vans," Buddy explained. "You want me to send them packing like the other one?"

"Yeah. And as soon as they're gone, Paige and I'll be leaving to go to the main house."

Suddenly, there was no other place Paige wanted to be. She inched closer and caught a glimpse of the van. It was indeed one that reporters used, and it was from a local station out of San Antonio.

The rain was still heavy, making it hard to see, and the only light came from the van's headlights. Buddy didn't get out of his truck. As he'd done with Jax and her, he lowered the window. The passenger's window on the van lowered, too.

And that's when Paige saw the gun.

Chapter Sixteen

"Get down!" Jax shouted to Buddy.

He did see Buddy duck down on his truck's seat, but Jax had no idea if it was in time. Because a split second later, there was another sound that Jax didn't want to hear.

A shot rang out.

Damn.

The shot hadn't come from Buddy, either, but whoever was inside that reporter's van. Jax seriously doubted it was reporters, and it sure as heck wasn't the Moonlight Strangler.

So who was it?

"Oh, God," Paige said, moving closer to the window. "Was Buddy hit?"

But Jax didn't have the answer to that. Not yet. However, he couldn't just stand here while Buddy was killed right in front of him.

He texted Buddy. And waited. The seconds crawled by with no answer. So Jax tried Hank next. He got an answer right away, but it wasn't an answer he liked.

What the devil's going on down there? Hank wanted to know.

I'll let you know when I know, Jax texted back.

"Get the gun from the closet in the bedroom," Jax instructed Paige. She'd know exactly where it was since it was where she'd left it before she moved out. "When you get back, I want you to stay inside and stay down."

She started to move, then stopped and frantically shook her head. "You can't be thinking about going out there."

Jax didn't have time to argue. "Just get the gun, and we'll go from there."

Thankfully, she hurried off to do that while Jax kept watching out the window. No more shots. And he couldn't see either Buddy or the shooter. Buddy was smart, so maybe he was playing dead, hoping the shooter would get out so that Buddy could return fire.

Because of the van's blinding headlights and the rain, Jax couldn't see through the windshields of either vehicle. However, there was likely at least two people in the van because the shot had come from the passenger's-side window.

Without taking his attention off the vehicles, Jax pressed in Jericho's number. There were ranch hands nearby, but Jax might need Jericho to coordinate the communication so that no one was hurt from friendly fire.

"There's trouble," Jax said the moment Jericho answered. "A van just pulled up in front of my house, and someone inside fired a shot at Buddy." He rattled off the license plate number to Jericho. "We might need an ambulance."

Jericho cursed. "Where are you and Paige now?"

"Inside my house, but I'm about to go outside and see if I can sneak up on the people inside the van. Just let everyone know what's going on so the main house is all locked up. Text me if you need to tell me anything and make sure I have some backup ASAP."

"I will. Don't guess it'd do any good to tell you to wait. No, I'll save my breath," Jericho added before Jax could say anything. "Just be careful."

"I will. Hank's nearby, too, so you should probably call him first. I don't want him coming down here into the middle of this. Not until I figure out what *this* is, anyway. But if he spots me, I want him to cover me."

Just as Jax was finishing up the call with Jericho, Paige came running back into the room with not just one gun but with two. And she had some extra magazines of ammo, as well.

"Any sign of Buddy yet?" she asked. She tried to peer out the window, but Jax moved her back behind him.

He shook his head and tried to figure out the best way to do this. If he waited, Buddy could die. And if he didn't wait, the same might happen.

Jax made brief eye contact with her. Just enough to let her see that this was not a negotiable situation. "I'm going outside to get a better look at what's going on. Once I'm out the door, I want you to arm the security system. The code is 4031. Then I want you to hide and not come out until I tell you it's safe."

"No," Paige repeated several times during his instructions.

But Jax didn't even try to bargain with her. He dropped a kiss on her mouth and hurried to the back door, grabbing his black Stetson along the way. He turned off the alarm and shot her a glance to remind her of what she needed to do.

"I'll be right back," he said, giving her another kiss.

Jax ignored the pleading look in her eyes, and he stepped out the door and onto the back porch. He didn't move, though, until he heard her press in the code to set the alarm.

Good.

At least if anyone tried to break through any of the windows or doors, the alarm would go off.

He went to the side of the porch by the swing where they'd found the camera and jumped down to the ground. It'd been raining long enough that the ground was soggy, and the water and mud oozed over his boots. The rain wouldn't help with visibility, but it could give him an advantage.

If he couldn't see them, then maybe they wouldn't be able to see him, either.

Ducking down and using the cruiser for cover, Jax looked around. He still didn't have a good view of the van because of Buddy's truck, so he hurried closer, sandwiching himself between the house and the cruiser. At least this way, no would sneak up on him from behind, but that left sides he had to cover.

He checked the cruiser door. Locked, of course. And he cursed himself for not grabbing the keys from the kitchen counter. That could turn out to be a bad mistake. Maybe, though, when Jericho arrived, he could open it using a remote. That would give Jax a bullet-resistant shield in case this turned into a gunfight.

There was no sign of Hank, but that didn't mean the ranch hand wasn't out there somewhere. And he wouldn't be alone. Soon, Jericho would have others around. He hoped Weston and Chase would stay in the main house with Matthew. Jax didn't want backup if it meant putting his son at risk.

Since the angle was still wrong for Jax to see what was going on, he crawled beneath the cruiser. The ground was wet here, too, and the rain soaked straight through his clothes. However, when he came out on the other side, he finally had the viewpoint he needed.

And his heart slammed against his chest.

No. This couldn't be happening. The back door of the van was wide open.

Hell.

There was no telling how many gunmen could have gotten out of there by now. They could have used the ditches or even Buddy's truck for cover so they could get closer to the houses.

He texted Buddy again, hoping the man would respond so he could tell Jax just how bad this threat was.

But still no answer. Jax prayed that was because Buddy was still playing dead and not because he actually was.

Jax's phone dinged before he could put it away, and he saw Jericho's name on the screen. Hank's behind the center barn but can't see you. I'm on the way.

Hurry, Jax texted back, because he was certain he was going to need help. And soon.

"Jax?" someone called out. "Don't shoot. It's me." And it was a voice he instantly recognized.

Belinda.

A dozen thoughts went through his head. There was no reason for her to be here. No good one, anyway. But there was one bad reason.

Was Belinda the person who'd been trying to kill Paige and him?

It sickened him to think it was her, someone who'd been so close to him and his family. But Jax pushed all of that aside so he could deal with this.

"Come out so I can see you," Jax demanded.

He didn't expect her to obey that order. And that's why he was surprised when she did.

With the rain sheeting down in front of the van's headlights, he saw the movement. Then the person stepped out, not from the back but rather from the driver's seat.

It was Belinda all right.

And she started walking straight toward him.

PAIGE HAD FOLLOWED Jax's orders to a tee. Except for one thing. One thing he wasn't going to like.

She hadn't hidden as he'd wanted. She couldn't. Not with him out there facing heaven knew what.

One of the first things she'd done after faking her death was to take firearms training. It had meant overcoming a lot of old fears, but she'd managed it, and that training might be needed now to help Jax.

She kept to the side of the window in the living room, and she continued to glance out. Nothing.

Well, not at first.

Then she'd heard Belinda call out to Jax, and Paige had known that this situation was about to take an ugly turn.

Paige readied her gun when Belinda came out from behind the wheel of the van. Belinda was wearing a light-colored dress that stood out in the darkness, and when she came out in full view and started walking toward the cruiser, Paige realized something was missing.

Belinda wasn't carrying a gun.

And with the way the rain was making her dress cling to her body, it would be next to impossible for her to have a concealed weapon.

Still, why was she here? And why had she been driving that van?

And where was Jax?

Paige was sure he was out there somewhere, but she'd lost sight of him after he'd jumped off the porch.

Judging from the sound of his voice when he'd called out to Belinda, he was still somewhere near the house. Paige prayed he had taken cover, because while

Belinda might not be armed, someone in that van certainly was. And that person had shot at Buddy.

"Jax?" Belinda said again. She kept walking, her hands stiff as boards by her sides, her focus on the cruiser. If she felt the rain whipping at her, she didn't have any reaction to it.

"Did you shoot Buddy?" Jax asked. "Did you hurt him?" Definitely near the cruiser. Or maybe under it.

Belinda shook her head, but there was no outcry of innocence. She seemed dazed, or else she was pretending to be. This could all still be her doing. Some kind of ruse to draw Jax out, but if so, why wasn't Belinda trying to do the same to Paige? The woman hated her, not Jax.

Didn't she?

Maybe Belinda wanted Jax to suffer because he'd allowed his ex-wife back in his life. Except he hadn't really done that—despite what'd happened earlier in the kitchen. There'd been no reconciliation. But perhaps Belinda didn't know that.

Belinda stopped when she was still about five yards from the cruiser, and since she was still in the path of those van headlights, it was easier for Paige to see her. Easier for Paige to take aim at her, too.

And that's what Paige did.

"Buddy's hurt, I think," Belinda finally said. She sounded as woozy as she looked, and she wobbled a little. She made an uneasy glance over her shoulder. "You don't have much time. You have to do this before Jericho and the others get here."

"What do we have to do?" Jax challenged.

"I'm supposed to give you a message." The woman made yet another glance over her shoulder. "If Paige comes out right now and surrenders, then no more bullets will be fired."

Everything inside Paige went still. *Surrender.* Somehow, she'd known it would come down to this. Whoever was in that van wanted her dead.

Darrin or Leland.

Of course, Belinda could be faking this, too. That way, she could pretend someone else was behind it so she could get Paige out of the picture while allowing herself to get back in Jax's good graces one day.

"Who told you to give me that message?" Jax asked.

Belinda shook her head again. "I'm not sure." Her gaze darted around again. "He was wearing a mask. All four of them were wearing masks, and only one did all the talking. I didn't recognize his voice."

Oh, mercy. If Belinda was telling the truth, then there were four hired killers practically on their doorstep. Except one of them might have been the person doing the hiring, if Belinda hadn't.

"Buddy needs medical attention," Belinda went on. "I'm supposed to tell you that an ambulance can come right away as soon as Paige gets in the van."

"That's not going to happen," Jax shouted. Not to Belinda. The message was no doubt meant for the men in the van. "And what about you? What happens to you in this so-called plan?" Jax added. Now, that was addressed to Belinda.

Belinda appeared to be fighting back tears. "They said I could stay here, that I'd be all right." The fight against the tears—whether real or pretend—was a fight that Belinda lost, and she started to sob.

"Hurry up!" someone yelled. "Quit your crying and tell him the rest now." A man. And he wasn't inside the van. It sounded as if he was much closer to the house.

Paige's breath stalled in her throat. Was someone about to break in?

The security alarm would go off if a window broke or if someone came in through the door, but it'd be too late by then. She'd find herself in the middle of a gunfight.

"I don't want them to hurt Matthew," Belinda sobbed.

"Tell him the rest now," the man repeated.

It took Belinda a couple of seconds to speak, and even then she continued to sob. "If Paige doesn't come out now and surrender, there's a gunman near the main house. He climbed out through the back of the van and made his way there on foot. He's got a rifle, and he has orders to start shooting."

Paige's breath didn't just stall. It vanished.

No.

This couldn't be happening.

"Paige?" the man called out.

He sounded even closer than before. Maybe on the front porch, though she hadn't seen him move from the van to there.

"I'm not giving you any more time," the man yelled.

"If you're not out of that house in five seconds, your son will pay for it."

Paige had no doubts, none, that he was telling the truth. Her little boy was in danger. Jax, too. And the only chance she had of stopping it was to go out there.

"Paige, no!" Jax shouted. "Don't do it."

But she was already on the move.

She disarmed the system so the alarm wouldn't sound. Paige wanted to be able to hear the monster who was responsible for this. She wanted to try to kill him before he did any damage.

With her gun gripped in her hand, Paige threw open the door and stepped out onto the front porch.

Chapter Seventeen

This was not what Jax wanted. He wanted Paige in the house, out of the line of fire, but here she was out in the open. Worse, judging from the sound of the hired gun's voice, he was somewhere in the front yard.

No doubt waiting to grab her. Or kill her.

Jax had to do something to stop that.

He scrambled out from the cruiser, keeping close to the house, and ran to the front porch as fast as he could. He didn't call out for Paige because he didn't want the gunman or anyone inside that van to try to take him out before Jax got to her.

The moment he reached the porch, he grabbed hold of Paige and pulled her to the ground. He wasn't able to break her fall, which meant he'd probably hurt her, but it was better than her being out in the open and gunned down.

Someone fired a shot, and it blasted into the house right behind them. Another inch, and it would have hit Jax in the head. Jax pushed Paige even lower, until she was flat against the ground, and he lay across her, trying to protect her. He prayed it would be enough.

"I had to come out here," Paige insisted. "To protect Matthew. Belinda said there was a shooter in place."

"I'm pretty sure that was a bluff. There are a dozen men patrolling the grounds around the house. They wouldn't let a shooter get that close."

He hoped.

And while he was hoping, Jax added that if shots were indeed fired there, Matthew and the others would be safe in the playroom at the center of the house. Certainly, Jericho had alerted the family to trouble, and they would go in there.

Paige shook her head. "I just panicked."

Heck, so had he. Hearing his son threatened like that had made him want to tear these fools limb from limb. And he still might do that before the night was over. But for now, Jax needed to do some damage control.

First, he checked to see if Belinda had gotten down on the ground. She had. If she was innocent in all of this, he didn't want her caught in the cross fire, and if she was guilty, he didn't want her in a good position to try to shoot at them or call out orders to those thugs.

Of course, Jax hadn't seen a gun anywhere on her, and she didn't appear to be wearing any kind of communicator. That still didn't mean she wasn't calling the shots for this fiasco.

"Without lifting your head," Jax whispered to Paige, "try to keep an eye on Belinda."

Paige nodded and maneuvered beneath him just enough so she could do that. "Is Jericho coming?"

"He should be here any minute." In fact, maybe he

was already there. Jax wasn't sure if his brother was going to do a quiet approach or not.

And it was quiet right now.

Too quiet.

Jax listened, trying to pick through the sounds of the rain and make sure that hired thug wasn't trying to sneak up on them. However, he didn't hear any footsteps, but he heard voices coming from the van.

Someone—two men from the sound of it—seemed to be arguing.

Maybe that would work in their favor. If the shooters were distracted, Jax could maybe do something about that idiot at the front of the house.

Jax moved, trying to keep his body in front of Paige in case the shots started again. He could still hear the two men arguing, and he hoped it was distracting the guy in the front. Jax crawled to the edge of the porch, looked around. But didn't spot him.

Where the hell was he?

And Jax hoped that he wasn't trying to make his way to the main house.

Jax was so focused on looking for the goon that the sound of the gunshot startled him. His heart jumped to his throat.

Paige.

Had the goon shot her?

He couldn't look behind him fast enough. But she was all right and looking as confused and worried as he was. Jax hoped that she would realize the shot hadn't gone anywhere near the main house. This one was much, much closer.

"Got one of them," someone called out. "I'm pretty sure this one's dead. He was trying to sneak up on you from the back porch."

Hank.

Thank God. The last Jax had seen of Hank, he'd been in his truck, but obviously he'd gotten out and moved closer to the house. Good.

One down. Three to go.

Or maybe four if Belinda was involved.

However, Jax was beginning to believe she was a victim in all of this. She was still sobbing, so either she was innocent or she regretted this stupid, dangerous plan that'd been set into motion. A plan that might have already killed Buddy.

"Jericho," Paige said, and she motioned toward the end of the road.

Jax looked in that direction and saw the flash of the blue lights. Obviously his brother had decided not to go with the quiet approach. Maybe it would spur the arguing men to use the van to try to get away.

They wouldn't.

Not while they were sandwiched between Jericho and Jax. Still, it would get them away from Paige, and he wanted her as far from the gunfire as possible. And it was likely that van was loaded with enough firepower to do some serious damage. Not good. Because as long as this fight went on, they were all in danger, and an ambulance wouldn't be able to get to Buddy.

In case the gunmen stayed put and made their stand here, Jax knew he had to get Paige to better cover. He tossed her his phone. "Text Jericho. See if he can open the cruiser."

Paige gave a shaky nod and fired off the text. They waited. Not long. And she shook her head. "He's too far away. But he's going to drive closer."

Maybe that wouldn't take long. Because Jax heard something that put a knot in his stomach.

Silence.

The men were no longer arguing. By now, they must have seen the lights of Jericho's cruiser, and they were no doubt ready to do whatever it was they'd come here to do.

Jax hurried back to Paige. "Stay low and move toward the cruiser. Fast. The second Jericho unlocks it, get inside."

They'd hardly made it a foot when the next shot came. It slammed into the ground way too close to them.

"Keep moving," Jax told Paige, and he turned, hoping to see the shooter.

No such luck, but since he had the extra ammo in his jeans pocket, Jax fired a shot directly into the windshield of the van. The bullet didn't shatter the glass. Didn't stop the shooter, either.

Because the shots started coming, and not just from one angle. All three of the remaining gunmen were shooting, not just at them. Plenty of those shots were going in Jericho's direction.

Thankfully, Paige just crawled, and Jax followed, trying to pinpoint the exact location of at least one of the gunmen so he could try to send a shot his way.

And then Jax heard it.

Not the sound of the shots. Nor of the gunmen. Even with the slap of the rain against his hat, Jax heard the voice coming from the van.

"Daddy."

Hell, no.

It was Matthew.

PAIGE FROZE, THE sound of her baby's voice slamming through her as hard as a bullet. Oh, God.

Had they kidnapped him?

Were they going to hurt him to try to draw her out?

Matthew's voice came again, the sound slicing through her. "Daddy."

She started to scramble toward the van, but Jax caught on to her and pulled her right back to the ground. This time, though, he didn't cover her with his body. He maneuvered them to the cruiser, and they ducked behind it.

But Paige didn't want to stop there. She had to keep moving. Had to get to her son.

Everything inside her was screaming for her to help Matthew. It didn't help that her little boy's voice kept coming from that van. Repeating that one word.

Daddy.

It sounded like a plea for help.

Were they hurting him?

Jax took hold of her chin, forcing eye contact with

her. "It's a recording. It has to be. Think this through. If these men had taken Matthew, someone at the house would have texted me."

Paige had to fight through the panic to let that sink in. Jax was right. Unless, of course, the absolute worst had happened—that these monsters had managed to break into the main house, kill or incapacitate everyone inside and then kidnap Matthew.

"We would have heard gunfire," Jax added, as if he'd known exactly what she was thinking. "The ranch hands wouldn't have let anyone that close to the house without there being gunfire."

True. And she remembered that someone had planted the camera with an eavesdropping device on the porch swing. Paige had seen Belinda out there on that very swing with Matthew. At some point Matthew could have said, "Daddy," and the device could have recorded it.

And these monsters were using it now to torture Jax and her.

It'd almost worked. Paige had nearly bolted out there, and that was almost certainly what this killer wanted her to do.

"Matthew!" Belinda shouted. "You can't hurt him. Please don't hurt him."

Paige couldn't see the woman, but she understood the sheer panic and terror that Belinda was likely feeling. And that didn't sound fake.

"Damn. Belinda's running out there," Jax mumbled.

Belinda screamed when there were more shots, and

Paige flattened herself on the ground so she could look beneath the cruiser.

Unlike Jax.

He was no longer down but rather peering over the trunk. Paige wanted to shout for him to get down, but she saw the movement from the corner of her eye.

Someone scrambled toward Belinda, and she hoped it was Hank. No such luck. It was a man dressed all in black, and he was wearing a ski mask. He grabbed hold of Belinda's hair, dragging her to a standing position in front of him, and he hauled her backward until they were against the detached garage.

And the thug put the gun to Belinda's head.

For the first time since this latest nightmare had started, Paige actually hoped that Belinda was part of this. If so, she was safe. Her own hired gun wouldn't shoot her. But if she was innocent, then she was in grave danger. She'd been a loose end that these men might want to tie up by murdering her.

"The boss man says you probably won't care a rat about me holding the nanny at gunpoint," the man behind Belinda shouted. "But I figure a lawman's a lawman to the core, and you aren't going to just hide behind that cop car or your badge and let me put a bullet in her head."

He was calling Jax out. But why? Why did they want Jax dead?

Maybe they didn't.

Perhaps the plan was to separate Jax from her. Either way, he could be hurt or killed, and Paige wasn't going to stay put and let that happen.

"What do you want?" she called out.

That earned her a glare from Jax. "Just stay quiet. Jericho should be close enough soon to unlock the cruiser."

Paige had no idea when that would happen. At least one of the gunmen was still shooting at Jericho, and while his cruiser would be bullet-resistant as well, it wasn't bulletproof, and some of those shots would eventually tear through the cruiser and get through.

Jericho and whoever was inside could be shot.

And all that could happen while Buddy was bleeding out.

"I have to do something to end this fast," Paige told Jax, and even though he was cursing at her, Paige repeated her shouted question. "What do you want?"

Paige had expected the thug holding Belinda to start doling out their demands. Demands that would almost certainly involve her surrender. Not exactly a surprise since they'd already demanded it when she'd been inside the house.

"What do I want?" a man shouted back. "I want *you*."

Not the guy behind Belinda. This voice came from the van, and it was a voice she had no trouble recognizing.

Leland.

Chapter Eighteen

Jax wasn't surprised that Leland was behind these attacks, but he wouldn't have been taken aback if it'd been Darrin, either. Of course, maybe the two were working together.

After all, Darrin could be the one shooting at Jericho. Or even the one calling the shots.

"I'm so sorry," Paige whispered.

"Don't," Jax snapped, and he hated that she even felt the need to apologize. Hated his harsh tone even more.

She probably thought he was blaming her for this, too. The way he'd blamed her for nearly getting killed by the Moonlight Strangler.

But he wasn't.

Jax was blaming himself. He had seen the anger in Leland. Had felt it. And he hadn't been able to do a damn thing to stop it.

"Stop shooting at Jericho," Paige called out to Leland. "And tell me what you want from me."

Jax doubted the shots would stop. But they did. Good. Maybe that meant he could reason with Leland, after all. Or perhaps it would give Jericho a chance to shoot both Leland and the other gunman in the van. Either way, Jax would take it.

"I want you to come out from hiding," Leland said, his voice a little closer now. Jax glanced around the cruiser and saw why.

Leland was out of the van and had made his way to the front of it. Not out in the open, exactly. He was using the van for cover, but it might make him an easier shot for Jericho or even Hank.

Wherever he was.

Jax hadn't heard a peep from the ranch hand since he'd managed to shoot one of the hired guns.

"I love you, Paige. I never wanted you dead," Leland added, sounding as unhinged as Jax figured he was. He'd always known that Leland was wrapped too tight, and the man had obviously lost it.

"Really? You never wanted me dead?" Paige answered, her voice filled with fear and some sarcasm. "Because it doesn't seem that way. Your hired thugs tried to kill us—twice."

"That wasn't the plan. The plan was only to kill Jax."

So he'd been the target. That felt like a punch to Jax. He was the reason Paige had nearly died. Of course, that reasoning was coming from the mind of a sick man. One in a rage because he was jealous.

"Were you working with the Moonlight Strangler?" Jax tossed out there.

"Hell, no." Leland didn't hesitate even a second,

and judging from the venom in his voice, he hated the serial killer as much as Jax did. Something they actually had in common.

Well, along with his feelings for Paige.

But Jax pushed those feelings aside right now. Later, he'd deal with them and what'd happened between them in the kitchen. For now, he couldn't let those thoughts and emotions get in the way.

"Is Belinda part of this?" Jax asked.

"Are you kidding me? She's in love with you, you fool. That bitch has fought me every step of the way, though I'm betting she wouldn't mind if Paige died tonight. That's not gonna happen, though."

"I don't want anyone dead," Belinda shouted. "Please, just stop all of this."

"For once, I agree with her," Leland spat out. "I've done everything I could to win Paige, and it didn't work."

"Did you put that camera there?" Belinda, again. "Because they were trying to accuse me of doing it. I only touched it."

"Yeah, yeah. I put it there so I could hear and see what was going on. I waited until you took the kid out to see the horses, and I just waltzed right in and did it. I figured if anyone found it, they'd blame the Moonlight Strangler."

They had. At first. And with Belinda's print on there, it had definitely put her under suspicion.

"Did you send me the texts, too?" Paige asked.

Jax hated that she'd even spoken to the man. He could practically feel the rage coming off him.

"Yes," Leland finally answered. "I sent those texts to set up a meeting. I thought if I could just get you alone, someplace private, I could talk some sense into you. That's why I had my men set the fire near the road, too. It was all about getting you away from him." The volume of his voice got louder with each word. "I didn't know the real Moonlight Strangler was going to get involved. And not just involved with contacting Paige, but going after Belinda, too."

Jax believed him, about that, anyway. There was no reason for Leland to have the Moonlight Strangler mark Belinda as his next victim. And if Leland really wanted Paige for himself, he wouldn't have put her in the path of a serial killer. But that's exactly what he'd done, because his attacks had alerted the Moonlight Strangler that Paige was still alive.

"Enough of this. We have a grenade launcher," Leland went on. "And my man's got it aimed at Jericho. Tell your brother to stop moving that cruiser forward, or we'll blast him and his deputy to smithereens. The same will happen if he even tries to shoot us."

Damn.

Jax wanted to believe that was a bluff, but he seriously doubted it. No, Leland would have come prepared, and this was almost certainly the way he planned to escape with Paige.

But Jax wasn't going to let that happen.

She'd nearly died once from an encounter with a

violent killer, and Jax hadn't been able to stop it. Somehow, he would stop this one.

"Or maybe you'd rather we aim the grenade launcher at the main house?" Leland went on. "It's not what I want to do, Paige, but I will if you don't cooperate."

Jax had no idea of the range on the launcher, but he doubted it could deliver a grenade all the way to the main house. Still, he didn't want to risk it.

"Since you want me dead," Jax shouted to the man, "why don't I come out instead of Paige. You want to punish her, right? Punish her for coming back to me. Well, here's your chance. You can punish her by killing me and then keeping her alive so she'll have to live with it."

Now it was Paige who glared at him. "You're not sacrificing yourself."

That wasn't what he had in mind, but whatever he did at this point would carry that risk. A risk that would be worth it.

"I just want to do something to get Leland out of cover so I can shoot him," Jax told her.

That was true. For the most part. He did want to shoot Leland, but Leland was a cop, too, and no doubt had just as good of an aim as Jax.

"I want you dead, all right," Leland answered. "But no deal. Paige is coming with me."

Jax didn't see that with a happy ending. Leland might not kill Paige right off, but it would eventually happen.

"You really think you can just leave here and have

a life with Paige?" Jax fired back. "The law would be looking for you."

"Maybe. It wasn't supposed to happen this way." Leland cursed. "I was supposed to be out of here without anyone seeing me, and then Darrin would take the fall."

"Darrin?" Paige and Jax asked at the same time.

"Is he with you right now?" Jax pressed.

"No. He's not here. He's at his place in San Antonio. Darrin's *committing suicide* right about now from a drug overdose. He has a history of drug abuse, and his medical records will prove it. But I guess he'll be dying for nothing. Still, the world won't miss a pig like that."

That was a serous example of the pot calling the kettle black. Yeah, Darrin was a pig, but Leland was a killer. Darrin, maybe Buddy, too, and heaven knew how many others would be dead before this was over.

Unless Jax ended it now.

Jax still didn't have a clean shot, not even close, but it would have to do. He levered himself up just enough so he could see over the trunk of the cruiser. And he took aim.

But before Jax could even pull the trigger, the shot blasted through the air.

PAIGE COULDN'T SEE what was happening, but she had no trouble hearing the shot. Or the one that followed.

Not ones that Jax or Leland had fired, either.

These bullets had come from the direction where that hired gun had hold of Belinda.

Belinda screamed, a blood-curdling sound that cut

through even the blasts of gunfire. And for several horrifying moments, Paige thought the thug had shot the woman.

He hadn't.

Someone had shot the thug.

The man dropped like a stone, his gun splatting onto the soggy ground beside him.

That's when Paige saw someone. *Jericho*. He came out from the side of the detached garage, his gun still aimed at the fallen man. Jericho hooked his other arm around Belinda and dragged her back behind the garage.

But how had Jericho gotten there? No one had come out of the cruiser. No one that she'd seen, anyway. Of course, it was dark and raining, and it was hard to see much of anything.

Or maybe he'd never even been in the cruiser.

He could have sneaked out at the end of the road and had the deputy drive it closer. If so, it was a smart plan, and it had likely saved Belinda's life.

However, Leland clearly wasn't happy about it.

"No!" Leland shouted. "You can't do this to me. Launch the grenade now."

Oh, God. Paige hadn't forgotten about that particular threat, but she hadn't realized Leland would use it so quickly. She didn't even have time to say a word, not that it would have stopped Leland anyway, before the cracking sound came from the opened back doors of the van.

Followed by the blast.

Much, much louder than a gunshot, and the cruiser exploded into a fireball. It lit up the night sky and sent fiery debris falling down all over the road and yard.

Paige's heart stopped. Whoever was inside there had to be dead. And Leland wasn't finished.

Yelling at the top of his lungs, Leland turned, taking aim at Belinda and Jericho. He fired four shots, nonstop. Just as Jericho pulled Belinda to the ground.

Paige had no idea if Jericho had gotten Belinda, or himself, out of the path of those bullets in time, but it was possible there were four injured or dead people: Buddy, Jericho, Belinda and the deputy in the cruiser.

"Stay down," Jax warned her when she moved to try to see Jericho.

Jax came up again and fired his Glock right at Leland. Judging from the profanity that Jax mumbled, he missed.

But Leland kept shooting, and so did the hired gun who had launched that grenade into the cruiser.

"Wait here," Jax said. "And I mean it. I need to get a better angle so I can stop Leland."

She caught on to his arm when he started to move. Paige wanted to beg him not to go out there, but time wasn't on their side here. They needed to end this fast so the ambulance could get onto the grounds. Still, it crushed her to think that Jax might be hurt or worse.

"Be careful," was all she managed to say.

That was it. And Jax was gone.

He lowered himself to the ground, crawling toward the front porch. Away from cover and directly toward

Leland. Leland had finally stopped firing at Jericho, but a few seconds later, she realized that was probably because he was reloading. The shots soon picked up again.

"We've got one more grenade," Leland shouted. "Paige, this is your last chance. I know you're behind the police car by the house. And that's exactly where the next grenade would go. It'll take out both Jax and you."

Her breath stalled in her throat, and the panic started to rise again. The grenade could do that. As big as that other blast had been, it'd take out them and the house, and maybe hurt Jericho and Belinda, too.

But maybe she could save Jax.

Maybe.

She wasn't just going to give up. She'd done that once when the Moonlight Strangler had left her for dead, and she wasn't doing that again. If she had to die, she wanted to at least die fighting.

Paige came up off the ground, ready to try to shoot Leland. But there was another shot. Not one that Jax had fired, either. She saw Jericho, and he was no longer by the garage with Belinda. He was closer to the road where the cruiser was still blazing. And Jericho had shot into the van.

Hopefully, he'd killed the man about to launch that grenade at them.

But there was no time for Paige to figure that out now. Leland was alive, and he could still do plenty of damage.

Paige took aim at Leland, but Leland saw her and pivoted in her direction. Ready to kill her.

And Paige pulled the trigger first.

She missed.

But Jax didn't.

Jax was already in place, and he sent two shots straight into Leland's chest. Everything seemed to stop. Including Leland. He stood there, frozen, his blank gaze connecting with hers for what seemed an eternity before he collapsed.

"Stay here," Jax warned her.

Not that she could move, anyway. Paige wasn't sure she had enough breath for that, and her legs were shaking. The rest of her body, too.

Jax hurried to Leland, kicking aside the man's gun and checking for any signs of life. "He's dead," Jax called out.

On the back side of the van, Jericho did the same thing to the thug he'd shot. "This one, too."

Jax didn't stay near Leland. He ran to Buddy's truck and looked inside. "Get an ambulance here *now*!"

Chapter Nineteen

Lucky.

That was the one word that kept going through Jax's mind.

They'd gotten damn lucky tonight. And while he hated to rely on something as fragile as luck, he'd take it. Things had gotten bad, but they could have been a whole lot worse.

The proof of that was right in front of him.

Paige was sitting on the floor of the playroom at the main house, and she was holding Matthew. Their son was sacked out, but Paige kept holding him, anyway. Probably because it helped settle her nerves. Well, as much as anything could settle them after the ordeal they'd been through.

Jax looked up the hall when he heard the footsteps. Jericho was making his way toward him, and his brother was finishing up yet another phone call. Something that Jax had been doing on and off as well for the past two hours since all hell had broken loose. Those two hours hadn't done much to take that stark look out of Paige's eyes, but maybe nothing could do that.

Paige and Matthew weren't alone in the room. Alexa and his mom were still there. Both were pretending to watch a movie they'd put on before Matthew fell asleep. Before the other kids dozed off, too. But Alexa and his mother looked more shell-shocked than anything else.

There'd been several good things that had come out of this mess. Good things other than just them all being in one piece. Leland and his hired guns were dead.

All of them.

And as Jax had learned later, there'd been no one in the cruiser that Leland's thug had blown up. Jericho had gotten out at the end of the road and walked up. Before the explostion, Dexter had slipped out through the back and into a ditch. Hank was all right, as well. Not a scratch on him.

Jax couldn't say the same for Buddy, though.

"Anything from the hospital yet?" Jax asked when Jericho was closer.

Jericho nodded. "Buddy's out of surgery. The bullet collapsed his lung, and he'll be out of commission for a couple of weeks. Buddy said to let you know that it'll only be a couple of days."

It would be weeks. Jax would make sure of it, though it would be hard to make the ranch hand stick to resting.

"What about Belinda?" Jericho asked.

"She's shaken up but on the way to her sister's in

San Antonio. She'll come back tomorrow to give her statement, but she said Leland kidnapped her."

Jericho made a sound of agreement. "That's what she told me, too, when I had her by the side of the garage. I figure Leland was using her as a decoy, but he would have killed Belinda if he'd managed to get his hands on Paige."

Definitely.

They'd gotten lucky all right.

"I don't think Belinda will be coming back to the ranch, or even to her house for that matter," Jax added a moment later. And he couldn't blame her. Besides, Belinda had to know that Paige would be staying around.

At least Jax hoped that was Paige's plan.

He frowned.

What was her plan, anyway?

"I asked about Cord when I was talking to the doctor," Jericho went on, snaring Jax's attention. "No change, but Cord's already complaining about having to stay in the hospital. I figure he'll sneak out first chance he gets."

Cord wouldn't if Addie had anything to say about it. And she would. It was obvious that she loved Cord like a brother. Because he was just that. Still, it stung a little, and Jax wasn't even sure why. It wasn't as if he'd had his only sister to himself over the years. He'd always shared her with his other brothers. Adding one more to the mix didn't seem like a big deal, but it was.

It was something he was definitely going to have to get over.

"No change in the Moonlight Strangler's condition, either," Jericho went on. "The doc said that's not good, that the longer he's in the coma, then the chances are that he'll stay that way for the rest of his miserable life."

Which meant they'd never be able to question him. They'd never be able to ask him why he'd murdered all those women.

Of course, he probably wouldn't have told them, anyway. Killers rarely spoke the truth, and the bottom line was the Moonlight Strangler might be just an ordinary sociopath with no real motive for murder. Not a motive that would make sense to anyone else, anyway.

Paige glanced up at Jax, maybe because she'd heard him mention the killer, but she didn't get up and join Jericho and him in the conversation. Which was good. She didn't need to hear any more details about the man who'd made her life a living hell.

"How long will the Moonlight Strangler be at the hospital?" Jax asked. Because it was only about fifteen miles from the ranch.

Too damn close.

Of course, a million miles was too close. Jax wanted the killer as far away as possible from Paige and the rest of his family, and he wanted that to happen yesterday.

"The doc thinks they can transfer him to the prison hospital as early as tomorrow," Jericho answered. "His condition is stable, and they can better guard him there than in Appaloosa Pass."

Agreed. A monster like that needed to be behind layers and layers of bars and security.

"What about Darrin?" Jax continued.

Jericho shook his head. "He didn't make it. By the time the ambulance got to his house, he'd been dead for a half hour or longer."

Another of Leland's victims. It was hard for Jax to feel sorry for the man who'd caused Paige so much pain, but Darrin didn't deserve to be murdered.

Jericho tipped his head to Paige. Her attention was still fixed on Matthew. "How's she holding up?"

Jax was about to put that *shaken up* label on her the way he had Belinda. And she was indeed shaken to the core. But she was also tough as nails. She'd gone straight from nearly being killed by a crazy cop to the main house to see Matthew. Paige had even managed to give their son a smile and make this seem like playtime.

"How are you holding up?" Jericho pressed. "And how are you *holding up* with Paige?"

There it was. Jericho's famous ESP. Jericho's tone let him know that he was certain that Jax and she had become lovers again.

Jax lifted his shoulder. "I'm not sure." And sadly it was true. Yeah, they had indeed become lovers again, but Jax wasn't sure if that was because of their feelings for each other or because it'd been just sex and a good release for tension.

Paige glanced at him again.

Jax knew what he wanted it to be—much more than just sex, that was for sure—but it was hard to undo all the arguments that had torn them apart. And there was her lie about being dead.

That suddenly didn't seem so big in the grand scheme of things.

"Want my advice?" Jericho asked, but he didn't wait for Jax to answer. "You should have sex with her again."

Jax gave him a flat look.

But Jericho only flashed him that all-knowing brotherly half smile. "I know people say that sex messes with your head, but sometimes it can make things a whole lot clearer."

Yes. It could.

And it had for him.

However, this wasn't something Jax intended to keep discussing with Jericho. Even if it was good advice.

"I don't expect the family just to welcome Paige back with open arms," Jax said, speaking more to himself than Jericho now.

"Well, you sure as hell should, considering how you feel about her." With that, Jericho gave him a pat on the back and strolled away.

Now Paige got to her feet. She kissed Matthew on his cheek, eased him onto the quilt that had been stretched on the floor and made her way to Jax.

"Is everything okay?" she asked.

Jax considered giving her a summary of all the updates he'd just gotten from Jericho, but that could wait. Because he thought they could both use it, he slipped his arm around her waist, eased her to him. And he kissed her.

Man, he wasn't sure how she managed, but every kiss with Paige felt like the first one. Even though there'd been a ton of them in between the first one and now.

The kiss went on a little longer than Jax had planned. Mainly because she tasted so good and because Paige slipped right into the kiss, and his arms, as if she could spend the rest of the night doing just this.

And maybe they could.

He stopped the kiss only because he heard his mother clear her throat. Jax looked into the playroom, expecting to have to dole out a lukewarm apology for carrying on in front of her. He darn sure wasn't about to apologize for the kiss itself, though.

But his mother was smiling. Alexa, too.

Jax hadn't especially needed the green light from either of them, but he'd take it, and he moved Paige out of the doorway and into the hall so they could have some privacy.

He kissed her again. And again.

His plan was to make her mind a little cloudy and to remind her of this heat between them. Of course, in doing that, he also reminded himself.

"You saved my life tonight," she whispered against his mouth. "Today, too," she added. And just like that, she shuddered, the flashbacks no doubt getting through the haze of the kiss.

Jax pulled her back to him. "I'm a cop. It's my job." He tried for it to sound like a joke, and she managed a little smile. But the smile didn't quite make it all the way to her eyes.

But the tears did, and she started blinking them back. "I'm so sorry—"

No way did he want to hear this, so he gave her one more kiss. Jax made it long and deep, and he pressed her against the wall, body to body, so that she'd remember some other things that didn't have to do with killers and bullets.

He kissed her so long that he thought maybe his lungs were about to burst. They broke apart, both of them gasping for air.

"I don't need an apology," he assured her. "None of this was your fault. Or mine. Let's pin this right on Leland and leave the blame there, agreed?"

"But I was a fool to let him get so close to me."

Ah, hell. This was going to take more than just a kiss. "You're not a fool," he assured her.

Jax let go of her just long enough to step back to the playroom. "Could you watch Matthew for a while?" he asked his mom. "I need to…chat with Paige."

He hadn't meant to pause in the middle of that, and it made it sound as if he had something sexual on his mind.

Which he did.

"Of course," his mother said, smiling. "Take your time."

Jax went back to Paige, taking hold of her hand and leading her up the stairs. To the guest room. He got her inside, shut the door and kissed her before she could ask any questions or attempt another apology.

"Is that to convince me I'm not a fool?" she asked, breathless again.

"More or less. Less," he settled on saying. He lowered the kiss to her neck.

Then to her breasts.

Finally, he got the results he wanted. That silky sound. Her face flushed, and he could see her pulse on her throat. All good signs. So was the fact that she latched on to him and dragged him back for another kiss.

And then she dragged him to the floor.

He was mindful of all her bruises and scrapes, but she wasn't. Paige pulled him on top of her.

There it was again. That raging fire. The timing for it sucked since she was probably dealing with a bad adrenaline crash, but maybe there was no bad time for sex when it came to them.

She reached between them and unhooked his holster, dropping it on the floor next to them, and she went after his shirt. He wanted this. Wanted her naked, too.

But then Jax froze.

But he also wanted a heck of a lot more.

"I'm in love with you," he said, but then shook his head. "I'm *still* in love with you."

Considering she had him half naked and looked like

sex on a silver platter, he was surprised at the soft smile she managed. Not a trace of lust in it. Well, just a little trace. There was always some heat whenever they looked at each other.

"Good, because I'm still in love with you, too." She paused. "And I want to move back home with Matthew and you. I want to make up for all the time I lost with both of you."

He nodded in approval. That was the best news he'd heard all day. Maybe in his entire life. "You'll have to marry me again, though. Just so I can make an honest woman out of you."

She smiled, too, at his lame joke. "And I can make an honest man out of you."

Judging from her next kiss, it wasn't that kind of honesty she had on her mind. It wasn't on Jax's, either. But when they were done here, he was getting Paige back to the altar ASAP.

"Oh, and I want more kids," she added, breaking the kiss only long enough for her to speak those few but very important words.

"Agreed." He wanted more, too, and at the rate they were going, they'd have one in under a year. Heck, they might be starting one tonight. "Anything else on your wish list?"

She smiled. "Just you, Jax. Just you."

That was his cue to kiss her like he meant it. Which he did. Jax also worked on getting her naked, and he kissed all those places he was uncovering.

"One day we're going to actually make it to the bed," Paige whispered, unzipping him.

"We'll work our way there together." And Jax kissed her again so they could get started on their new-old life together.

* * * * *

USA TODAY *bestselling author Delores Fossen's*
APPALOOSA PASS RANCH
miniseries continues next month with
LAYING DOWN THE LAW.
Look for it wherever
Harlequin Intrigue books are sold!

THE MONTANA HAMILTONS *Series*
by B.J. Daniels goes on.
Turn the page for a sneak peek at INTO DUST...

CHAPTER ONE

THE CEMETERY SEEMED unusually quiet. Jack Durand
paused on the narrow walkway to glance toward the
Houston skyline. He never came to Houston without
stopping by his mother's grave. He liked to think of
his mother here in this beautiful, peaceful place. And
he always brought flowers. Today he'd brought her fa-
vorite: daisies.

He breathed in the sweet scent of freshly mown lawn
as he moved through shafts of sunlight fingering their
way down through the huge oak trees. Long shadows
fell across the path, offering a breath of cooler air. For-
tunately, the summer day wasn't hot and the walk felt
good after the long drive in from the ranch.

The silent gravestones and statues gleamed in the
sun. His favorites were the angels. He liked the idea
of all the angels here watching over his mother, he
thought, as he passed the small lake ringed with trees
and followed the wide bend of Braes Bayou situated
along one side of the property. A flock of ducks took

flight, flapping wildly and sending water droplets into the air.

He'd taken the long way because he needed to relax. He knew it was silly, but he didn't want to visit his mother upset. He'd promised her on her deathbed that he would try harder to get along with his father.

Ahead, he saw movement near his mother's grave and slowed. A man wearing a dark suit stood next to the angel statue that watched over her final resting place. The man wasn't looking at the grave or the angel. Instead, he appeared to simply be waiting impatiently. As he turned...

With a start, Jack recognized his father.

He thought he had to be mistaken at first. Tom Durand had made a point of telling him he would be in Los Angeles the next few days. Had his father's plans changed? Surely he would have no reason to lie about it.

Until recently, that his father might have lied would never have occurred to him. But things had been strained between them since Jack had told him he wouldn't be taking over the family business.

It wasn't just seeing his father here when he should have been in Los Angeles. It was seeing him in this cemetery. He knew for a fact that his father hadn't been here since the funeral.

"I don't like cemeteries," he'd told his son when Jack had asked why he didn't visit his dead wife. "Anyway, what's the point? She's gone."

Jack felt close to his mother near her grave. "It's a sign of respect."

His father had shaken his head, clearly displeased with the conversation. "We all mourn in our own ways. I like to remember your mother my own way, so lay off, okay?"

So why the change of heart? Not that Jack wasn't glad to see it. He knew that his parents had loved each other. Kate Durand had been sweet and loving, the perfect match for Tom, who was a distant workaholic.

Jack was debating joining him or leaving him to have this time alone with his wife, when he saw another man approaching his father. He quickly stepped behind a monument. Jack was far enough away that he didn't recognize the man right away. But while he couldn't see the man's face clearly from this distance, he recognized the man's limp.

Jack had seen him coming out of the family import/ export business office one night after hours. He'd asked his father about him and been told Ed Urdahl worked on the docks.

Now he frowned as he considered why either of the men was here. His father hadn't looked at his wife's grave even once. Instead he seemed to be in the middle of an intense conversation with Ed. The conversation ended abruptly when his father reached into his jacket pocket and pulled out a thick envelope and handed it to the man.

He watched in astonishment as Ed pulled a wad of money from the envelope and proceeded to count it.

Even from where he stood, Jack could tell that the gesture irritated his father. Tom Durand expected everyone to take what he said or did as the gospel.

Ed finished counting the money, put it back in the envelope and stuffed it into his jacket pocket. His father seemed to be giving Ed orders. Then looking around as if worried they might have been seen, Tom Durand turned and walked away toward an exit on the other side of the cemetery—the one farthest from the reception building. He didn't even give a backward glance to his wife's grave. Nor had he left any flowers for her. Clearly, his reason for being here had nothing to do with Kate Durand.

Jack was too stunned to move for a moment. What had that exchange been about? Nothing legal, he thought. A hard knot formed in his stomach. What was his father involved in?

He noticed that Ed was heading in an entirely different direction. Impulsively, he began to follow him, worrying about what his father had paid the man to do.

Ed headed for a dark green car parked in the lot near where Jack himself had parked earlier. Jack dropped the daisies, exited the cemetery yards behind him and headed to his ranch pickup. Once behind the wheel, he followed as Ed left the cemetery.

Staying a few cars back, he tailed the man, all the time trying to convince himself that there was a rational explanation for the strange meeting in the cemetery or his father giving this man so much money.

But it just didn't wash. His father hadn't been there to visit his dead wife. So what was Tom Durand up to?

Jack realized that Ed was headed for an older part of Houston that had been gentrified in recent years. A row of brownstones ran along a street shaded in trees. Small cafes and quaint shops were interspersed with the brownstones. Because it was late afternoon, the street wasn't busy.

Ed pulled over, parked and cut his engine. Jack turned into a space a few cars back, noticing that Ed still hadn't gotten out.

Had he spotted the tail? Jack waited, half expecting Ed to emerge and come stalking toward his truck. And what? Beat him up? Call his father?

So far all Ed had done from what Jack could tell was sit and watch a brownstone across the street.

Jack continued to observe the green car, wondering how long he was going to sit here waiting for something to happen. This was crazy. He had no idea what had transpired at the cemetery. While the transaction had looked suspicious, maybe his father had really been visiting his mother's grave and told Ed to meet him there so he could pay him money he owed him. But for what that required such a large amount of cash? And why in the cemetery?

Even as Jack thought it, he still didn't believe what he'd seen was innocent. He couldn't shake the feeling that his father had hired the man for some kind of job that involved whoever lived in that brownstone across the street.

He glanced at the time. Earlier, when he'd decided to stop by the cemetery, he knew he'd be cutting it close to meet his appointment back at the ranch. He prided himself on his punctuality. But if he kept sitting here, he would miss his meeting.

Jack reached for his cell phone. The least he could do was call and reschedule. But before he could key in the number, the door of the brownstone opened and a young woman with long blond hair came out.

As she started down the street in the opposite direction, Ed got out of his car. Jack watched him make a quick call on his cell phone as he began to follow the woman.

CHAPTER TWO

THE BLONDE HAD the look of a rich girl, from her long coiffed hair to her stylish short skirt and crisp white top to the pale blue sweater lazily draped over one arm. Hypnotized by the sexy swish of her skirt, Jack couldn't miss the glint of silver jewelry at her slim wrist or the name-brand bag she carried.

Jack grabbed the gun he kept in his glove box and climbed out of his truck. The blonde took a quick call on her cell phone as she walked. She quickened her steps, pocketing her phone. Was she meeting someone and running late? A date?

As she turned down another narrow street, he saw Ed on the opposite side of the street on his phone again. Telling someone…what?

He felt his anxiety rise as Ed ended his call and put away his phone as he crossed the street. Jack took off after the two. He tucked the gun into the waist of his jeans. He had no idea what was going on, but all his instincts told him the blonde, whoever she was, was in danger.

As he reached the corner, he saw that Ed was now only yards behind the woman, his limp even more pronounced. The narrow alley-like street was empty of people and businesses. The neighborhood rejuvenation hadn't reached this street yet. There was dirt and debris along the front of the vacant buildings. So where was the woman going?

Jack could hear the blonde's heels making a *tap, tap, tap* sound as she hurried along. Ed's work boots made no sound as he gained on the woman.

As Ed increased his steps, he pulled out what looked like a white cloth from a plastic bag in his pocket. Discarding the bag, he suddenly rushed down the deserted street toward the woman.

Jack raced after him. Ed had reached the woman, looping one big strong arm around her from behind and lifting her off her feet. Her blue sweater fell to the ground along with her purse as she struggled.

Ed was fighting to get the cloth over her mouth and nose. The blonde was frantically moving her head back and forth and kicking her legs and arms wildly. Some of her kicks were connecting. Ed let out several cries of pain as well as a litany of curses as she managed to knock the cloth from his hand.

After setting her feet on the ground, Ed grabbed a handful of her hair and jerked her head back. Cocking his other fist, he reared back as if to slug her.

Running up, Jack pulled the gun, and hit the man with the stock of his handgun.

Ed released his hold on the woman's hair, stumbled

and fell to his knees as she staggered back from him, clearly shaken. Her gaze met his as Jack heard a vehicle roaring toward them from another street. Unless he missed his guess, it was cohorts of Ed's.

As a van came careening around the corner, Jack cried "Come on!" to the blonde. She stood a few feet away looking too stunned and confused to move. He quickly stepped to her, grabbed her hand and, giving her only enough time to pick up her purse from the ground, pulled her down the narrow alley.

Behind them, the van came to a screeching stop. Jack looked back to see two men in the front of the vehicle. One jumped out to help Ed, who was holding the blonde's sweater to his bleeding head.

Jack tugged on her arm and she began to run with him again. They rounded a corner, then another one. He thought he heard the sound of the van's engine a block over and wanted to keep running, but he could tell she wasn't up to it. He dragged her into an inset open doorway to let her catch her breath.

They were both breathing hard. He could see that she was still scared, but the shock seemed to be wearing off. She eyed him as if having second thoughts about letting a complete stranger lead her down this dark alley.

"I'm not going to hurt you," he said. "I'm trying to protect you from those men who tried to abduct you."

She nodded, but didn't look entirely convinced. "Who are you?"

"Jack. My name is Jack Durand. I saw that man

following you," he said. "I didn't think, I just ran up behind him and hit him." It was close enough to the truth. "Who are *you*?"

"Cassidy Hamilton." No Texas accent. Nor did the name ring any bells. So what had they wanted with this young woman?

"Any idea who those guys were or why they were after you?"

She looked away, swallowed, then shook her head. "Do you think they're gone?"

"I don't think so." After he'd seen that wad of money his father had given Ed, he didn't think the men would be giving up. "I suspect they are now looking for both of us." When he'd looked back earlier, he'd thought Ed or one of the other men had seen him. He'd spent enough time at his father's warehouse that most of the dockworkers knew who he was.

But why would his father want this woman abducted? It made no sense and yet it was the only logical conclusion he could draw given what he'd witnessed at the cemetery.

"Let's wait a little bit. Do you live around here?"

"I was staying with a friend."

"I don't think you should go back there. That man has been following you for several blocks.".

She nodded and hugged herself, looking scared. He figured a lot of what had almost happened hadn't yet registered. Either that or what had almost happened didn't come as a complete surprise to her. Which made him even more curious why his father would want to abduct this woman.

ED URDAHL COULDN'T believe his luck. He'd picked a street that he knew wouldn't have anyone on it this time of the day. On top of that, the girl had been in her own little world. She hadn't been paying any attention to him as he'd moved up directly behind her.

The plan had been simple. Grab her, toss her into the van that would come speeding up at the perfect time and make a clean, quick getaway so no one would be the wiser.

It should have gone down without any trouble.

He'd been so intent on the woman in front of him, though, that he hadn't heard the man come up behind him until it was too late. Even if someone had intervened, Ed had been pretty sure he could handle it. He'd been a wrestler and boxer growing up. Few men were stupid enough to take him on.

The last thing he'd expected was to be smacked in the back of the head by some do-gooder. What had he been hit with, anyway? Something hard and cold. A gun? The blow had knocked him senseless and the next thing he'd known he was on the sidewalk bleeding. As he'd heard the van engine roaring in his direction, he'd fought to keep from blacking out as whoever had blindsided him had gotten away with the blonde.

"What happened?" his brother Alec demanded now. Ed leaned against the van wall in the back, his head hurting like hell. "I thought you had it all worked out."

"How the hell do I know?" He was still bleeding like a stuck pig. "Just get out of here. *Drive!*" he yelled at the driver, Nick, a dockworker he'd used before for less-than-legal jobs. "Circle the block until I can think of what to do."

Ed caught a whiff of the blonde's perfume and realized he was holding her sweater to his bleeding skull. He took another sniff of it. *Nice.* He tried to remember exactly what had transpired. It had all happened so fast. "Did you see who hit me?" he asked.

"I saw a man and a woman going down the alley," Alec said. "I thought you said she'd be alone?"

That's what he had thought. It had all been set up in a way that should have gone off like clockwork. So where had whoever hit him come from? "So neither of you got a look at the guy?"

Nick cleared his throat. "I thought at first that he was working *with* you."

"Why would you think that?" Ed demanded, his head hurting too much to put up with such stupid remarks. "The son of a bitch coldcocked me with something."

"A gun. It was a gun," Alec said. "I saw the light catch on the metal when he tucked it back into his pants."

"He was carrying a gun?" Ed sat up, his gaze going to Nick. "Is that why you thought he was part of the plan?"

"No, I didn't see the gun," Nick said. "I just assumed he was in on it because of who he was."

Ed pressed the sweet-smelling sweater to his head and tried not to erupt. "Are you going to make me guess? Or are you frigging going to tell me who he was?"

"Jack Durand."

"What?" Ed couldn't believe his ears. What were the chances that Tom Durand's son would show up on this particular street? Unless his father had sent him? That made no sense. *Why pay me if he sent his son?*

"You're sure it was Jack?"

"Swear on my mother's grave," Nick said as he drove in wider circles. "I saw him clear as a bell. He turned in the alley to look back. It was Jack, all right."

"Go back to that alley," Ed ordered. Was this Tom's backup plan in case Ed failed? Or was this all part of Tom's real plan? Either way, it appeared Jack Durand had the girl.

CASSIDY LOOKED AS if she might make a run for it at any moment. That would be a huge mistake on her part. But Jack could tell that she was now pretty sure she shouldn't be trusting him. He wasn't sure how much longer he could keep her here. She reached for her phone, but he laid a hand on her arm.

"That's the van coming back," he said quietly. At the sound of the engine growing nearer, he signaled her not to make a sound as he pulled her deeper into the darkness of the doorway recess. The van drove slowly up the alley. He'd feared they would come back. That's why he'd been hesitant to move from their hiding place.

Jack held his breath as he watched the blonde, afraid she might do something crazy like decide to take her chances and run. He wouldn't have blamed her. For all she knew, he could have been in on the abduction and was holding her here until the men in the van came back for her.

The driver of the van braked next to the open doorway. The engine sat idling. Jack waited for the sound of a door opening. He'd put the gun into the back waistband of his jeans before he'd grabbed the blonde, thinking the gun might frighten her. As much as he wanted to pull it now, he talked himself out of it.

At least for the moment. He didn't want to get involved in any gunplay—especially with the young woman here. He'd started carrying the gun when he'd worked for his father and had to take the day's proceeds to a bank drop late at night. It was a habit he'd gotten used to even after he'd quit. Probably because of the type of people who worked with his father.

After what seemed like an interminable length of time, the van driver pulled away.

Jack let out the breath he'd been holding. "Come on. I'll see that you get someplace safe where you can call the police," he said and held out his hand.

She hesitated before she took it. They moved through the dark shadows of the alley to the next street. The sky above them had turned a deep silver in the evening light. It was still hot, little air in the tight, narrow street.

He realized that wherever Cassidy Hamilton had been headed, she hadn't planned to return until much later—thus the sweater. He wanted to question her, but now wasn't the time.

At the edge of the buildings, Jack peered down the street. He didn't see the van or Ed's green car. But he also didn't think they had gone far. Wouldn't they expect her to call the police? The area would soon be crawling with cop cars. So what would Ed do?

A few blocks from the deserted area where they'd met, they reached a more commercial section. The street was growing busier as people got off work. Restaurants began opening for the evening meal as boutiques and shops closed. Jack spotted a small bar with just enough patrons that he thought they could blend in.

"Let's go in here," he said. "I don't know about you, but I could use a drink. You should be able to make a call from here. Once I know you're safe…"

They took a table at the back away from the television over the bar. He removed his Stetson and put it on the seat next to him. When Cassidy wasn't looking, he removed the .45 from the waistband of his jeans and slid it under the hat.

"What do you want to drink?" he asked as the waitress approached.

"White wine," she said and plucked nervously at the torn corner of her blouse. Other than the torn blouse, she looked fine physically. But emotionally, he wasn't sure how much of a toll this would take on her over the long haul. That was if Ed didn't find her.

"I'll have whiskey," he said, waving the waitress off. He had no idea what he was going to do now. He told himself he just needed a jolt of alcohol. He'd been playing this by ear since seeing his father and Ed at the cemetery.

Now he debated what he was going to do with this woman given the little he knew. The last thing he wanted, though, was to get involved with the police. He was sure Ed and his men had seen him, probably recognized him. Once his father found out that it had been his son who'd saved the blonde…

The waitress put two drinks in front of them and left. He watched the blonde take a sip. She'd said her name was Cassidy Hamilton. She'd also said she didn't know why anyone would want to abduct her off the street, but he suspected that wasn't true.

"So is your old man rich or something?" he asked and took a gulp of the whiskey.

She took a sip of her wine as if stalling, her gaze lowered. He got his first really good look at her. She was a knockout. When she lifted her eyes finally, he thought he might drown in all that blue.

"I only ask because I'm trying to understand why those men were after you." She could be a famous model or even an actress. He didn't follow pop culture, hardly ever watched television and hadn't been to the movies in ages. All he knew was, at the very least, she'd grown up with money. "If you're famous or something, I apologize for not knowing."

INTRIGUE

Available August 23, 2016

#1659 LAYING DOWN THE LAW
Appaloosa Pass Ranch • by Delores Fossen
DEA agent Cord Granger believes his father's a serial killer, but when the attacks continue after his father is arrested, Cord has no choice but to protect Karina Southerland, the killer's new target.

#1660 DARK WHISPERS
Faces of Evil • by Debra Webb
When attorney Natalie Drummond loses pieces of her memory and starts experiencing hallucinations, no one but B&C Investigations detective Clint Hayes believes the danger she's sensing is real.

#1661 DELIVERING JUSTICE
Cattlemen Crime Club • by Barb Han
A woman with no memory turns to millionaire cowboy Tyler O'Brien for help learning who she is and why someone is after her.

#1662 SUDDEN SECOND CHANCE
Target: Timberline • by Carol Ericson
As cold case reporter Beth St. Regis conducts an investigation into her own past, the secrets she unleashes force her to turn to FBI agent Duke Harper, a man she shares an intimate history with, for protection.

#1663 HOSTAGE NEGOTIATION
Marshland Justice • by Lena Diaz
After police chief Zack Scott rescues beautiful and determined Kaylee Brighton from her kidnapper, he must rely on her to bring her abductor to justice.

#1664 SUSPICIOUS ACTIVITIES
Orion Security • by Tyler Anne Snell
Orion Security's leader, Nikki Waters, has always been in charge. But when she becomes a stalker's obsession, she'll need her newest hire, bodyguard Jackson Fields, to keep her safe.

REQUEST YOUR FREE BOOKS!
2 FREE NOVELS PLUS 2 FREE GIFTS!

H HARLEQUIN®

INTRIGUE

BREATHTAKING ROMANTIC SUSPENSE

YES! Please send me 2 FREE Harlequin® Intrigue novels and my 2 FREE gifts (gifts are worth about $10). After receiving them, if I don't wish to receive any more books, I can return the shipping statement marked "cancel." If I don't cancel, I will receive 6 brand-new novels every month and be billed just $4.74 per book in the U.S. or $5.49 per book in Canada. That's a savings of at least 12% off the cover price! It's quite a bargain! Shipping and handling is just 50¢ per book in the U.S. and 75¢ per book in Canada.* I understand that accepting the 2 free books and gifts places me under no obligation to buy anything. I can always return a shipment and cancel at any time. Even if I never buy another book, the two free books and gifts are mine to keep forever.

182/382 HDN GH3D

Name _____ (PLEASE PRINT)

Address _____ Apt. #

City _____ State/Prov. _____ Zip/Postal Code

Signature (if under 18, a parent or guardian must sign)

Mail to the **Reader Service:**
IN U.S.A.: P.O. Box 1867, Buffalo, NY 14240-1867
IN CANADA: P.O. Box 609, Fort Erie, Ontario L2A 5X3
**Are you a subscriber to Harlequin® Intrigue books
and want to receive the larger-print edition?
Call 1-800-873-8635 or visit www.ReaderService.com.**

* Terms and prices subject to change without notice. Prices do not include applicable taxes. Sales tax applicable in N.Y. Canadian residents will be charged applicable taxes. Offer not valid in Quebec. This offer is limited to one order per household. Not valid for current subscribers to Harlequin Intrigue books. All orders subject to credit approval. Credit or debit balances in a customer's account(s) may be offset by any other outstanding balance owed by or to the customer. Please allow 4 to 6 weeks for delivery. Offer available while quantities last.

Your Privacy—The Reader Service is committed to protecting your privacy. Our Privacy Policy is available online at www.ReaderService.com or upon request from the Reader Service.

We make a portion of our mailing list available to reputable third parties that offer products we believe may interest you. If you prefer that we not exchange your name with third parties, or if you wish to clarify or modify your communication preferences, please visit us at www.ReaderService.com/consumerschoice or write to us at Reader Service Preference Service, P.O. Box 9062, Buffalo, NY 14240-9062. Include your complete name and address.

HI15

Natalie's car suddenly swerved. Tension snapped through
Clint. She barreled off the road and into the lot of a
supermarket, crashing broadside into a parked car.

His pulse hammering, Clint made the turn and skidded
to a stop next to her car. He jumped out and rushed to her.
Thank God no one was in the other vehicle. Natalie sat
upright behind the steering wheel. The deflated air bag
sagged in front of her. The injuries she may have sustained
from the air bag deploying ticked off in his brain.

He tried to open the door but it was locked. He banged
on the window. "Natalie! Are you all right?"

She turned and stared up at him. Her face was flushed
red, abrasions already darkening on her skin. His heart
rammed mercilessly against his sternum as she slowly hit
the unlock button. He yanked the door open and crouched
down to get a closer look at her.

"Are you hurt?" he demanded.

"I'm not sure." She took a deep breath as if she'd only just remembered to breathe. "I don't understand what happened. I was driving along and the air bag suddenly burst from the steering wheel." She reached for the wheel and then drew back, uncertain what to do with her hands. "I don't understand," she repeated.

"I'm calling for help." Clint made the call to 9-1-1 and then he called his friend Lieutenant Chet Harper. Every instinct cautioned Clint that Natalie was wrong about not being able to trust herself.

There was someone else—someone very close to her—she shouldn't trust. He intended to keep her safe until he identified that threat.

Don't miss DARK WHISPERS
by USA TODAY *bestselling author Debra Webb,*
available in September 2016 wherever
Harlequin® Intrigue books and ebooks are sold.

www.Harlequin.com

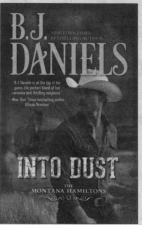